JAPANESE
TALES *of*
MYSTERY *and*
IMAGINATION

Edogawa Rampo (Hirai Taro, 1894–1965) is widely regarded as the father of Japanese mystery writing. Born in Mie Prefecture, he graduated in 1916 from Waseda University and took on a series of odd jobs, working as an accountant, clerk, salesman, and peddler of *soba* noodles from a cart, before discovering his vocation as a writer. The first modern writer of mysteries in Japan, and long-time president of the Japan Mystery Writers' Club, Rampo derived his pen name from the Japanese pronunciation of Edgar Allan Poe, under whose spell he fell early in his career.

EDOGAWA RAMPO

JAPANESE TALES of MYSTERY and IMAGINATION

translated by
JAMES B. HARRIS

with a new foreword by
PATRICIA WELCH

TUTTLE Publishing

Tokyo | Rutland, Vermont | Singapore

"Books to Span the East and West"

Tuttle Publishing was founded in 1832 in the small New England town of Rutland, Vermont [USA]. Our core values remain as strong today as they were then—to publish best-in-class books which bring people together one page at a time. In 1948, we established a publishing office in Japan—and Tuttle is now a leader in publishing English-language books about the arts, languages and cultures of Asia. The world has become a much smaller place today and Asia's economic and cultural influence has grown. Yet the need for meaningful dialogue and information about this diverse region has never been greater. Over the past seven decades, Tuttle has published thousands of books on subjects ranging from martial arts and paper crafts to language learning and literature—and our talented authors, illustrators, designers and photographers have won many prestigious awards. We welcome you to explore the wealth of information available on Asia at **www.tuttlepublishing.com**.

Published by Tuttle Publishing, an imprint of Periplus Editions (HK) Ltd.

www.tuttlepublishing.com

Copyright © 2012 Periplus Editions (HK) Ltd.
First edition, 1956

Library of Congress Cataloging-in-Publication Data

Edogawa, Ranpo, 1894-1965.
 [Short stories. English. Selections]
 Japanese tales of mystery and imagination / Edogawa Rampo; translated by James B. Harris; with a new foreword by Patricia Welch.
   222 p. : ill. ; 21 cm.
   ISBN 978-4-8053-1193-6 (pbk.)
1. Short stories, Japanese. I. Title.
PL826.D6A2 2012
895.6'34--dc23
          2011043079

ISBN 978-4-8053-1193-6

Distributed by

North America, Latin America & Europe
Tuttle Publishing
364 Innovation Drive, North Clarendon,
VT 05759-9436 U.S.A.
Tel: 1 (802) 773-8930; Fax: 1 (802) 773-6993
info@tuttlepublishing.com
www.tuttlepublishing.com

Japan
Tuttle Publishing
Yaekari Building, 3rd Floor, 5-4-12 Osaki,
Shinagawa-ku, Tokyo 141 0032
Tel: (81) 3 5437-0171; Fax: (81) 3 5437-0755
sales@tuttle.co.jp
www.tuttle.co.jp

Asia Pacific
Berkeley Books Pte. Ltd.
3 Kallang Sector #04-01, Singapore 349278
Tel: (65) 6741-2178; Fax: (65) 6741-2179
inquiries@periplus.com.sg
www.tuttlepublishing.com

Second edition
25 24 23 22   15 14 13 12 11   2203VP
Printed in Malaysia

Contents

Translator's Preface from the First Edition

EDOGAWA RAMPO, the author of Japanese mystery stories, who is making his debut in the English language with the publication of this book, enjoys wide popularity in Japan. Although the same cannot yet be said of him among mystery readers in America and Europe, he has already been frequently mentioned in American book reviews and commentaries as being, without question, the dean of Japanese mystery writers. In the words of Ina Telberg, who wrote of Edogawa Rampo in her article "The Japanese State of Mind" in the *Saturday Review of Literature*, "One of the most able exponents of the detective story in Japan is Edogawa Rampo, who heads the Japan Mystery Writers' Club. It is not improbable that if he is translated into English he may well enjoy here some of the popularity that the French Georges Simenon has had."

Ellery Queen, writing in his *Queen's Quorum* (1951) introduced Edogawa Rampo and his works as belonging to the period between Agatha Christie and Edgar Wallace in his listing of the world's most famous writers of short mystery stories. Queen also remarked that, "If you say the name Edogawa Rampo aloud, and keep repeating it, the name will seem to grow more and more familiar; and it should, because it is a verbal translation of the Japanese pronunciation of Edgar Allan Poe."

David Dempsey, in his column "In and Out of Books," run regularly in the *New York Times Book Review*, also commented on Rampo as follows: "Japan's most famous mystery story writer is named Edogawa Rampo. Rampo took this name because he is a great admirer of Poe. When a visiting American asked Kanji Hatano (a noted Japanese psychologist) if the Japanese reading public didn't confuse Rampo with the real Edgar Allan Poe, he replied, 'Oh, no . . . Edogawa Rampo is much more famous.'"

In the section devoted to pseudonyms in the introduction to Dashiell Hammett's *Woman in the Dark*, published by the Jonathan Press Mystery, Rampo was classified as belonging to the Vocal Method group, with the explanation that "When Hirai Taro (Edogawa Rampo's real name) decided to write under a nom de plume, he went back, with reverence and relevance, to the origin of the species . . . to the Father of the Detective Story . . ."

Edogawa Rampo was born October 21, 1894, in Nabari Town, Mie Prefecture, the son of a merchant who also practiced law. Most of his childhood was spent in Nagoya, but at the age of seventeen he went to Tokyo for higher studies. Entering Waseda University in 1912, he majored in economics and graduated with high honors four years later. During the next six years, Rampo tried his hand at diverse occupations, working successively as clerk for an import-export house, accountant at a shipbuilding yard, assistant editor of a newspaper, advertising solicitor, etc., etc. Frequently, between jobs, he followed the menial trade of peddling *soba*, or Japanese noodles, pulling the cart and blowing the eerie-sounding flute of the *soba* peddler, thus just managing to keep body and soul together.

It was not until 1923, the year of the great earthquake which devastated the whole of the Tokyo-Yokohama area, that Rampo discovered his real calling, i.e., writing mysteries. Until that time, no Japanese writer had attempted a modern detective story, although there did exist numerous translations of the works of Western writers.

In those days, only a single mystery magazine was in existence in the whole of Japan. This was the *Shin Seinen* which featured Japanese translations of the works of such Western mystery writers as Poe, Doyle, Chesterton, Freeman, and others.

Rampo, who had been an avid reader of American and European mysteries since his high school days, being jobless in Osaka at the time, mailed in to *Shin Seinen* a short mystery entitled "Nisen Doka" (The Two-Sen Copper Coin). Much to his surprise, the story was snapped up, and published by *Shin Seinen* side by side with the works of world-famous writers. Invited by the publishers to write more stories, Rampo readily complied, and as his reputation continued to grow by leaps and bounds as Japan's first spinner of modern mystery yarns, he finally went to Tokyo to pursue his new vocation in earnest.

During the thirty-one years up to the present, Rampo has written a total of twenty full-length books, fifty-three short stories and novelettes, ten full-length books for juveniles, and six volumes of essays devoted to the mystery story. The stories contained in this book are the best selections from Rampo's stock of short stories.

In introducing this noted Japanese mystery writer to the Western public, a brief resume of the mystery story in Japan is also in order. Old tales of court trials imported from China were the very first detective stories read in Japan. However, it was not until the year 1660 that a Japanese writer came under the spell of these Chinese classics and began to write stories of a similar nature.

During the next two centuries, various other writers turned out works along the same lines, the most famous of them being Saikaku Ihara's *Records of Trials Held Beneath a Cherry Tree*, published in the year 1689.

The next turning point came in the Meiji Period (1868–1912), when the Chinese-patterned detective story began to lose its popularity, and a new era of crime literature came into being with the rapid importation, translation, and sale of American, English, and French mystery classics. One of the earliest translators of these Western works into Japanese was Ruiko Kuroiwa, who from 1887 until the close of the century translated dozens of detective novels, thus introducing the modern Western crime story to Japanese readers. Among the many works which he translated into the Japanese language those of French writers predominated. Some fifteen or sixteen novels by Du Boisgobey, four novels by Gaboriau, as well as works by Wilkie Collins, A. K. Green, and others were translated by him and serialized in Japanese newspapers.

Subsequently, many other translators turned out numerous works by American and English writers, until finally, in the year 1923, the first original Japanese mystery story, Edogawa Rampo's "The Two-Sen Copper Coin," was born.

With the ice thus finally broken, a purely Japanese school of modern mystery fiction rapidly began to take shape, with the majority of the writers striving to give expression to their own original themes and ideas and adopting diverse styles rather than merely copying their Western predecessors and contemporaries. Thus, today, the Japan Mystery Writers' Club, which was founded by Edogawa Rampo, consists of a select membership of over one hundred professional writers of the purely Japanese school, who assiduously keep the Japanese mystery addicts supplied with an unlimited flow of mystery tales of every description.

A brief description of the manner in which this book was translated may also prove to be of interest to the reader, for it was undertaken under unique conditions. Edogawa Rampo, while fully capable of reading and understanding English, lacks the ability to write or speak it. On the other hand, the translator, a Eurasian of English-Japanese parentage, while completely fluent in spoken Japanese, is quite unable to read or write the language, as he was educated solely in English schools. Hence, for each line translated, the two collaborators, meeting once a week for a period of five years, were forced to overcome manifold difficulties in getting every line just right, the author reading each line in Japanese several times and painstakingly explaining the correct meaning and nuance, and the translator sweating over his typewriter having to experiment with sentence after sentence until the author was fully satisfied with what had been set down in English.

Whether or not this book will find a permanent place on the world's bookshelf of great mystery classics is a question that still remains to be answered, and the Occidental "whodunit" reader, currently flooded with large doses of jet-paced Mickey Spillane, may find Edogawa Rampo's typically Oriental tempo somewhat slow.

But whatever the reaction, it is Rampo's fervent hope that the publication of this book—the very first volume of collected Japanese tales of mystery and imagination ever to be published in the English language—may serve as the initial step towards placing original Japanese works on the list of the most popular mystery classics of the world.

James B. Harris
Tokyo, February 5, 1956

Foreword

Excess, Alienation and Ambivalence: Edogawa Rampo's Tales of Mystery and Imagination

by Patricia Welch

You mentioned your name as if I should recognize it, but I assure you that, beyond the obvious facts that you are a bachelor, a solicitor, a Freemason, and an asthmatic, I know nothing whatever about you. —Arthur Conan Doyle The Adventure of the Norwood Builder

The weird, the macabre and the mysterious have fascinated the imagination of man for generations. The reason for this fascination has, however, never been clearly defined—except that we are all a little frightened of the unknown…and yet attracted to it at the same time. —Peter Haining

Horror is that which cannot be made safe—evolving, ever-changing—because it is about our relentless need to confront the unknown, the unknowable, and the emotion we experience when in its thrall. —Douglas Winter

The Japanese writer Edogawa Rampo (1894–1965) has been called the Father of Japanese Mystery Fiction. This statement, while not inaccurate, fails to adequately consider examples of his writing that border on the macabre or the fantastic. While many of his works do feature conventional detection, his most memorable works tap into the elements of strangeness that Japan's headlong rush into modernity after the Meiji Restoration had unleashed. Far more than conventional mysteries, these stories incorporate elements of the fantastic, the gothic, and the absurd, in ways that thrill and entertain, but also leave the reader unsettled, as they delve deeply into the fear of the unknown that all humans share. For the Japanese of the early twentieth century, that unknown included not only the familiar monsters of the past, but also the monsters that were themselves born of modernity. Many of Rampo's most unforgettable works feature troubled city dwellers, their daily lives changed by the rapid transformation of material conditions, but still coming to terms with what these transformations meant on the level of subjectivity and interpersonal relationships. The self-reflective gaze through which he considers modern society surely resonated for his original readers. Rampo's prolific career began in the 1920s and extended to the end of his life, but only in recent years have readers outside Japan begun to seriously consider Rampo's work.

The name Edogawa Rampo is the pen name of Hirai Tarō, which, as commonly noted (by none other than Ellery Queen) resembles Edgar Allen Poe when said quickly. Rampo's choice of pen name reflects the Japanese writer's deliberate homage to the nineteenth-century American writer. But, as remarked by Mark Silver in *Purloined Letters: Cultural Borrowings in Japanese Crime Literature*, 1863–1937, the Chinese characters chosen to write the pen name can also be translated as "staggering drunkenly along the Edo River," or as I prefer, "chaotic ramblings."* The multiple levels of meaning that figure into the ideographs

---

* Hirai Tarō used the sobriquet Edogawa Rampo throughout his career; however, the characters that translate as "chaotic rambling" were used from his third work onward, suggesting even more strongly his self-conscious use of the name.

of his chosen pen name through sense and sound suggest that Rampo from the start saw his mission as a writer as multi-layered: first, as a conscious move to position himself as Japan's Edgar Allen Poe, and second to closely examine the contradictions of a life in modernity through his literary ramblings. The doubling of meaning, along with the slippages and gaps between his chosen pen name and its references further suggest the crucial anxieties of identity he, like other contemporary urban dwellers, experienced in his youth, a time of immense social change. Thus Rampo's pen name is a curiously apt moniker for a keen observer of the modern such as himself.

Rampo was born in the final years of the nineteenth century to a family with roots in Mie Prefecture, though he grew up mainly in the city of Nagoya in nearby Aichi Prefecture. Shortly before he entered the preparatory school for Waseda University, his family moved to Korea, then under colonial rule. He moved to Tokyo in September of that year. A year later, he entered Waseda University where he majored in economics. In the years that followed his 1916 graduation, he jumped from job to job, compiling a quirky resume that a millennial hipster would find impressive. Bouncing back and forth between Tokyo and Western Japan, he worked as a reporter, sold old books, edited a cartoon journal, toiled as a dock clerk and trader, and even—as the need arose—dishing out noodles at a cart. These diverse experiences surely provided Rampo with ample material as a writer.

While a university student, Rampo read detective stories by Poe, G. K. Chesterton, and Arthur Conan Doyle, which appealed to him precisely because of their use of careful plotting, logic and reasoning, and how their works made manifest the ultimately incomprehensible reservoirs of darkness that lie beneath the quotidian. While this suggests that Rampo took as a model the superbly intellectual and insightful detective figures prominent in most Golden Age Anglo-American detective fiction, it should be noted that the various "rules" of fair play for detective fiction that popularized the use of such detectives had yet to emerge in any systematic way.* An avid reader, he read as widely in the Japanese literary tradition as he did of the West's, and thus was versed in the Japanese classics, as well as in the tradition of moral crime tales popular in Japan through the Meiji Period. And as many have noted, he was equally familiar with Kuroiwa Ruikō's adaptations of Western crime fiction because his mother, a great fan, had read the best-selling author's works to him when he was a child. Even as a university student, he desired to travel abroad and write detective stories in the manner of Conan Doyle and Poe, but financial exigencies kept him at home.

Rampo came of age in the first decades of the twentieth century, at a time when Japan's victory in the Russo-Japanese War, early forays into Western-style Imperialism in Korea and Taiwan, and increased economic opportunities had helped to swell the population of large urban centers like Tokyo and Osaka. This contributed to the development of a small but growing middle class. In Tokyo, the descendants of Edokko (natives of Edo), *onoborisan* (domestic migrants) and university students jostled elbows as they struggled to establish identities for themselves in a rapidly evolving urban milieu where formerly fixed social categories involving gender and status no longer had the same weight they once had. The speed with which the urban population increased led to dramatic changes to Tokyo's increasingly urban landscape, and almost overnight what had been familiar started to disappear, only to be replaced again not many years later, in response to the newly emerging patterns of a capitalist life. Dreams of modern life were fed by an expanding consumer industry, epitomized by the growth of department stores, and

---

* S. S. Van Dine's "Twenty Rules for Writing Detective Stories" was first published in 1928, and signaled a decisive move to establish what its author felt proper for detective fiction, not necessarily what in fact contemporary readers encountered in their reading.

a constantly expanding array of magazines and journals targeted to particular groups. Modern girls, lauded and excoriated in the emerging mass media as *moga*, traded somber kimonos for more fashionable costumes, including—though still in the minority—Western dress. Urban youth attended movies, vaudeville shows, or engaged in so-called *ryōki* ("curiosity hunting"), needing ever more stimulation because they were no longer satisfied by the more sedate pleasures of old. Even academics got into the game: Kon Wajirō and others like him engaged in urban stalking in the name of *modernology*, a kind of social anthropology of the modern. As increasing numbers of train and subway lines spread the reach of the modern ever further, hybrid single-family "culture homes" began to displace both traditional *nagaya* tenements and larger multi-generational homes intensifying even further the pace of change.

In the words of William Gardner the 1920s were "the time when many of the hallmarks of modernity—urbanization, the experience of simultaneity, the proliferation of new media, the transformation of gender roles—occupied the center of national attention, and a diverse range of public voices vied to represent and define this modernity."* Through his early fiction, Rampo was one of these voices, though as an observer—not advocate. Fans avidly read what he wrote, captivated by his supreme ability to wed the logic of scientific inquiry and objectivity that characterized detective fiction with aspects of the grotesque and the erotic in ways that dug deeply into the subconscious fears and terrifying desires of his readers. Through the self-reflective gaze of his narrators and protagonists, readers came to look deeply at themselves and the contradictions in their lives. At precisely the same time that modernists and other writers were vying to represent and

---

* William O. Gardner. *Advertising Tower: Japanese Modernism and Modernity in the 1920s* (Cambridge: Harvard University Asia Center, 2006), 8.

define modernity, opposing forces were attempting to control and manage its expression, as Japan moved closer and closer to fascism and then total war.

Rampo's first story "The Two-Sen Copper Coin" (*Nisen dōka*) was published in the journal *Shinseinen* (*New Youth*) in 1923, launching both Rampo's prolific career and his association with the genesis of modern ratiocinative detective fiction in Japan. This story—on some levels a fairly direct reinterpretation of Edgar Allen Poe's story "The Gold Bug"—hinges on a coded message hidden inside a hollow coin. In it, two bored but impoverished university students are fascinated by the story of a thief who managed to brazenly steal the payroll envelopes of a large manufacturer of electrical products. Through fine detective work on the part of the police, the thief is quickly apprehended and brought to justice but never once does he speak of the whereabouts of the money. Soon, a reward for its return is offered. Utilizing his own considerable intellect, the narrator's roommate throws himself into the search for the missing money seemingly to the narrator's bemusement. In the conclusion, readers' expectations are shattered: they learn that though it appears that the roommate has located the hidden money through an accurate reading of the various clues, he is himself the subject of an elaborate game played on him by the narrator, which has in turn drawn in the story's readers. As Sari Kawana explains, the story "was praised . . . for observing some of the signature elements of detective fiction . . . while also overturning some of the central conventions of the genre. . . . Rampo completely dismantles the implicit assumption of the narrator as a sidekick to an able detective and a faithful chronicler of his friend's triumphs . . . In "*Nisen dōka*," the nameless *watashi* ("I") gets the last laugh, not only from his friend who took himself to be a great detective but also from the readers who expected his narrative to be sincere and complete."* Not merely a success with critics, it was popular with the publisher and general readers as well.

Following this auspicious debut, Rampo had a lengthy and varied career as a writer. He wrote dozens of works, including short stories, novels, and essays, and later in his career, numerous works intended primarily for juvenile readers. Many of his works have remained continually in print. A self-identified practitioner of *honkaku* (orthodox) detective fiction in the postwar years, he was also closely identified with prewar detective fiction's *henkaku* (fantastic) elements. The works that incorporate elements both bizarre and logical are most memorable to readers. His fascination with codes, disguises, doubling, inferiority complexes, optics, thrill seeking, sexual fetishes, and other dangerous desires appeal to readers then and now, by the way they foreground the unstable boundaries between self and other in a time of great change. Among Rampo's long list of published works, the following novels stand out: *Blind Beast*, (1929), *Demon of the Desert Isle* (1929–30), and *The Strange Tale of Panorama Island* (1926–7). These works employ such themes as impersonation, sado-masochism, and narcissistic obsession, within the framework of detection. Among his shorter works, the disturbingly creepy stories "The Human Chair," "The Red Chamber," "The Hell of Mirrors," and "The Caterpillar" deserve mention. In addition to his own literary creations, he was instrumental in the founding of the Japan Mystery Writers' Club and is also known for his 1961 memoir *Tantei Shōsetsu Yonjūnen* (*Forty Years of Writing Mystery Stories*). His contribution to the genre has been honored further by the institution of the Edogawa Rampo Prize in 1955, awarded annually to individuals who have furthered the detective genre in Japan.

---

* Sari Kawana. *Murder Most Modern: Detective Fiction and Japanese Culture* (Minneapolis: University of Minnesota Press, 2008), 20.

Unlike his contemporaries Kawabata Yasunari and Tanizaki Jun'ichirō, Rampo has not been well represented in English translation until recently, despite continuing popularity in his native land. As of 2005, this volume, originally published in 1956, was the only full-length translation to be found, although many of its stories were republished in other mystery and horror anthologies over the years. Since 2006, however, Kurodahan—a small publishing house in Japan—has published (or commissioned) no fewer than three of Rampo's full-length works, and has published an anthology containing short stories and essays. In addition, "The Caterpillar" and "The Traveler with the Pasted Rag Picture," two stories included within this volume, have been retranslated for inclusion in *Modanizumu: Modernist Fiction From Japan*, a new anthology of Japanese modernist fiction.* Further, reflecting a burgeoning interest in cultural productions of the 1920s and 1930s, including popular literature and detective fiction, a number of writers have begun to shed light on this important twentieth century author in a variety of scholarly works. And continuing a practice of creative reuse that began as early as 1927 with the film adaptation of his novel *The Dwarf*, contemporary creative artists in a variety of fields have revisualized Rampo's works, themes and characters for a variety of media, including film, manga, anime, and theater. Thus it is only fitting that Tuttle Publishing reissue the classic volume that introduced Rampo to Western readers. It contains many of his best stories, all but one of which was written in the 1920s.

The nine tales in this newly reissued edition of *Japanese Tales of Mystery and Imagination* will thrill and entertain, but will likely also linger on the minds of most readers as they delve deeply into the fear of the unknown that unites all humans. Each

---

* This valuable new collection also contains a fine translation of "The Two-Sen Copper Coin" mentioned previously.

deftly taps into the elements of strangeness that Japan's head-long rush into modernity had unleashed. Although Rampo was first praised for introducing Japanese readers to the logical detective story, what is perhaps more striking—at least to this reader—is how in the best stories extreme logic is conjoined with the erotic grotesque in a terrifying hybridity. In their shocking excess, many of the stories seem to defy the possibility of a fully rational existence, which the emerging contours of the new modern city seemed to suggest was possible. They do so by in the way they present otherness in its multiple forms, and in their ambivalence towards modernity and the West as reflected onto the objects and structures of daily life. We have bizarre tales that feature characters narcissistically obsessed with mirrors, doubling and substitution, and even a character whose self-identity is so filled with self-loathing that he literally disappears into the furniture. In others, the modern need for continual stimulation has led to greater and greater abuses of varying sorts. In some we see deep-seated anxieties related to the various changes wrought by Japan's modernization. We might speculate that the deployment of such themes in literature is a safe way to diffuse and sublimate the anxious, immoral, and criminal feelings hidden deep within us, particularly at a time, as in Japan of the 1920s, when "totems and taboos" (to paraphrase Freud) in the form of social mores and conventions had begun to break down in the face of immense social change. Part of the pleasure of reading these works is the shock of recognition of those deeply buried elements of the human psyche.

Be that as it may, I also posit that erotic grotesqueries of the sort found in many of Rampo's stories embody a type of resistance to an increasingly totalitarian society by their very existence. In the words of Jim Reichert,

> Erotic-grotesque cultural performance functioned as an
> indirect form of resistance against the totalitarian tenden-

cies exhibited by the Japanese state during the 1920s and 1930s . . . [Such] works were produced and consumed at a historical moment when Japanese citizens were bombarded by propaganda urging them to devote themselves to such "productive" goals as nation building and mobilization. In this context, the sexually charged, unapologetically "bizarre" subject matter associated with erotic-grotesque cultural products is reconstituted as a transgressive gesture against state-endorsed notions of "constructive" morality, identity, and sexuality.*

Indeed, this tension can be felt in most of the stories that comprise this collection. Earlier I wrote that a number of competing factions were attempting to represent and define what it meant to be modern in 1920s and 1930s Japan. Although detractors tried to minimize the relevance of erotic grotesque performance as nonsense, we should not forget the attitude of oppositionality to conventional mores and the dehumanizing logic of capitalism embodied in most of these works. Rampo's stories, through their deployment of freakish or deviant characters, suggest a world where psycho-sexual boundaries and behaviors are unstable, and thus unable to be fully contained within any externally-generated notion of constructive identity.

The title of this collection, *Japanese Tales of Mystery and Imagination,* provides a useful way of categorizing each of the nine stories contained within, though because many of Rampo's works could easily fit either category, one should not rely too strongly on this handy characterization. For the purpose of this introduction, however, the *Tales of Mystery* include "The Psychological Test" (1925), "The Cliff" (1950), "The Twins" (1924), and "Two Crippled Men" (1924) and the *Tales of Imagination* include "The Human Chair" (1925), "The Caterpillar"

---

* Jim Reichert. "Deviance and Social Darwinism in Edogawa Rampo's Erotic-Grotesque Thriller Kotō no oni" (*Journal of Japanese Studies,* 2001), 115.

(1929), "The Hell of Mirrors" (1926), and "The Traveler with the Pasted Rag Picture" (1929).

In their exposition, the four tales of mystery differ considerably from the generic conventions familiar to readers of twentieth century Anglo-American mystery writing. While each is replete with precise details of characters' movements and personal quirks and psychologies, barely to be seen is the clever detective whose immense intellect and unfailing logic unravels a mystery, thus symbolically restoring order to a world gone awry. In fact, only one of the stories ("The Psychological Test") features a detective figure: the redoubtable Kogorō Akechi, Rampo's famous sleuth, in one of his first appearances. Instead, Rampo inverts the normal pattern to reveals both crime and perpetrator at the outset, or engages the reader through some similar form of inversion. He relates a world where an over-reliance on intellect and logic may have led either to a crime, the perpetrator's downfall, or both.

In two of the four stories, an almost perfect crime is cracked because the perpetrator's arrogance led him to believe he could outsmart any possible opponent. For example, "The Psychological Test" is about a Waseda University student whose greed and misplaced pride leads him to murder, a crime he almost blithely believes will never be linked to him. "The Cliff," unusually presented as a dialogue between a woman and her younger husband, concerns the circumstances surrounding the death of her first husband. In the story titled "The Twins," a condemned killer tells his story of fratricide to a priest. And finally, in the story entitled "Two Crippled Men," a man, psychologically crippled by the knowledge that he had murdered a man while sleepwalking when he was a student, confesses his strange tale to his companion, a man he believes has been honorably crippled in war, only to learn a surprising secret. While it is true that each of these stories privileges scientific methodology and logical deduction to finally arrive at the "real story," they also show the fallibility of science/authority, as in the end, the "perps" are usually tripped up by the means by which they attempted to elude detection.

Many of these stories also incorporate notions of the mysterious double, or the fearsome other. This is perhaps most overtly presented in "The Twins," where the narrator himself answers the question as to why he killed his brother: ". . . as for me, the very reason for my wanting to kill him was that we were two persons in one. And how I *hated* my other half! I wonder whether you've ever had such a feeling of uncontrollable hatred, far more severe than that which you could feel against any person not closely related to you. And in my particular case it was still more so because we were twins and I was insane with jealousy." (page 144). His over-confident assertion that all was well after he killed his brother is belied by his increasing terror at his own mirrored image, a manifestation of his guilty conscience. Readers will find the *Tales of Mystery* satisfying on a number of levels, particularly in the way that they intellectually engage readers and put them in the role of the all-but-absent detective, and through the convoluted—but logical—twists, turns and tricks that the writer employs, even as they recognize the deeper social context of these stories.

By contrast the volume's *Tales of Imagination* satisfy on a different level altogether. These stories cannot be considered detective tales at all; rather they are psychological horror stories that exploit what Stephen King has called our "phobic pressure points" in *Danse Macabre*, his study of horror fiction and film from the 1950s through the 1980s.* In "The Human Chair," for example a popular woman writer receives a strange missive of love and self-loathing from a chairmaker who has taken up residence inside a chair. Exquisitely satisfying on this

---

* It should be repeated that many of Rampo's "authentic" detective tales also touch upon "phobic pressure points." For the stories in this collection, I believe this to be most true of "The Twins" and "Two Crippled Men."

level alone, the story also presents a masterful discourse on the chairmaker's ambivalence vis-à-vis Japan's modernization. "The Caterpillar,"—Rampo's only story to be censored despite an ongoing concern that his tastes were "unhealthy"—is the psycho-sexual story about the relationship between a war veteran so horribly crippled he is likened to a caterpillar and his once dutiful wife. Censored because authorities believed it to be an anti-war tale, it in fact cuts far deeper, by raises troubling questions about what it means to be human. In "The Hell of Mirrors" a narcissistic man obsessed and delighted with his reflection experiences the ultimate fright when he attempts to see himself more fully. And in the chillingly rendered "The Red Chamber," a social club where bored urbanites tell tales of horror, a new member's tale shocks existing members to the core in a most unexpected way. And finally, in the poignantly eerie "The Traveler With the Pasted Rag Picture," human figures in a picture made from kimono scraps appears almost alive when seen through inverted binoculars.

In short, the stories in this volume will appeal to readers today, just as they appealed to their original readers in Japan. Rampo's concern with alienation and identity, with the limits of sight and other senses, remains as important now as it did then. In a world characterized by increasing violence and chaos, by the disintegration of moral compasses and traditional social support systems, where each of us struggles with questions of identity and society, Rampo's compelling tales of dislocated urbanites in a rapidly changing world resonate deeply. Enjoy and be wary.

The Human Chair

Yoshiko saw her husband off to his work at the Foreign Office at a little past ten o'clock. Then, now that her time was once again her very own, she shut herself up in the study she shared with her husband to resume work on the story she was to submit for the special summer issue of *K—* magazine.

She was a versatile writer with high literary talent and a smooth-flowing style. Even her husband's popularity as a diplomat was overshadowed by hers as an author.

Daily she was overwhelmed with letters from readers praising her works. In fact, this very morning, as soon as she sat down before her desk, she immediately proceeded to glance through the numerous letters which the morning mail had brought. Without exception, in content they all followed the same pattern, but prompted by her deep feminine sense of consideration, she always read through each piece of correspondence addressed to her, whether monotonous or interesting.

Taking the short and simple letters first, she quickly noted their contents. Finally she came to one which was a bulky, manuscript-like sheaf of pages. Although she had not received any advance notice that a manuscript was to be sent her, still it was

[Certain archaic terms have been amended. Ed.]

not uncommon for her to receive the efforts of amateur writers seeking her valuable criticism. In most cases these were long-winded, pointless, and yawn-provoking attempts at writing. Nevertheless, she now opened the envelope in her hand and took out the numerous, closely-written sheets.

As she had anticipated, it was a manuscript, carefully bound. But somehow, for some unknown reason, there was neither a title nor a by-line. The manuscript began abruptly:

"Dear Madam: . . ."

Momentarily she reflected. Maybe, after all, it was just a letter. Unconsciously her eyes hurried on to read two or three lines, and then gradually she became absorbed in a strangely gruesome narrative. Her curiosity aroused to the bursting point and spurred on by some unknown magnetic force, she continued to read:

Dear Madam: I do hope you will forgive this presumptuous letter from a complete stranger. What I am about to write, Madam, may shock you no end. However, I am determined to lay bare before you a confession—my own—and to describe in detail the terrible crime I have committed.

For many months I have hidden myself away from the light of civilization, hidden, as it were, like the devil himself. In this whole wide world no one knows of my deeds. However, quite recently an odd change took place in my conscious mind, and I just couldn't bear to keep my secret any longer. I simply had to confess!

All that I have written so far must certainly have awakened only perplexity in your mind. However, I beseech you to bear with me and kindly read my communication to the bitter end, because if you do, you will fully understand the strange workings of my mind and the reason why it is to you in particular that I make this confession.

I am really at a loss as to where to begin, for the facts which I am setting forth are all so grotesquely out of the ordinary. Frankly, words fail me, for human words seem utterly inadequate to sketch all the details. But, nevertheless, I will try to lay bare the events in chronological order, just as they happened.

First let me explain that I am ugly beyond description. Please bear this fact in mind; otherwise I fear that if and when you do grant my ultimate request and *do* see me, you may be shocked and horrified at the sight of my face—after so many months of unsanitary living. However, I implore you to believe me when I state that, despite the extreme ugliness of my face, within my heart there has always burned a pure and overwhelming passion!

Next, let me explain that I am a humble workman by trade. Had I been born in a well-to-do family, I might have found the power, with money, to ease the torture of my soul brought on by my ugliness. Or perhaps, if I had been endowed by nature with artistic talents, I might again have been able to forget my bestial countenance and seek consolation in music or poetry. But, unblessed with any such talents, and being the unfortunate creature that I am, I had no trade to turn to except that of a humble cabinet-maker. Eventually my specialty became that of making assorted types of chairs.

In this particular line I was fairly successful, to such a degree in fact that I gained the reputation of being able to satisfy any kind of order, no matter how complicated. For this reason, in woodworking circles I came to enjoy the special privilege of accepting only orders for luxury chairs, with complicated requests for unique carvings, new designs for the back-rest and arm-supports, fancy padding for the cushions and seat—all work of a nature which called for skilled hands and patient trial and study, work which an amateur craftsman could hardly undertake.

The reward for all my pains, however, lay in the sheer delight of creating. You may even consider me a braggart when you hear this, but it all seemed to me to be the same type of thrill which a true artist feels upon creating a masterpiece.

As soon as a chair was completed, it was my usual custom to sit on it to see how it felt, and despite the dismal life of one of my humble profession, at such moments I experienced an indescribable thrill. Giving my mind free rein, I used to imagine the types of people who would eventually curl up in the chair, certainly people of nobility, living in palatial residences, with exquisite, priceless paintings hanging on the walls, glittering crystal chandeliers hanging from the ceilings, expensive rugs on the floor, etc.; and one particular chair, which I imagined standing before a mahogany table, gave me the vision of fragrant Western flowers scenting the air with sweet perfume. Enwrapped in these strange visions, I came to feel that I, too, belonged to such settings, and I derived no end of pleasure from imagining myself to be an influential figure in society.

Foolish thoughts such as these kept coming to me in rapid succession. Imagine, Madam, the pathetic figure I made, sitting comfortably in a luxurious chair of my own making and pretending that I was holding hands with the girl of my dreams. As was always the case, however, the noisy chattering of the uncouth women of the neighborhood and the hysterical shrieking, babbling, and wailing of their children quickly dispelled all my beautiful dreams; again grim reality reared its ugly head before my eyes.

Once back to earth I again found myself a miserable creature, a helpless crawling worm! And as for my beloved, that angelic woman, she too vanished like a mist. I cursed myself for my folly! Why, even the dirty women tending babies in the streets did not so much as bother to glance in my direction. Every time I completed a new chair I was haunted by feelings of utter despair. And with the passing of the months, my long-accumulated misery was enough to choke me.

One day I was charged with the task of making a huge, leather-covered armchair, of a type I had never before conceived, for a foreign hotel located in Yokohama. Actually, this particular type of chair was to have been imported from abroad, but through the persuasion of my employer, who admired my skill as a chair-maker, I received the order.

In order to live up to my reputation as a super-craftsman, I began to devote myself seriously to my new assignment. Steadily I became so engrossed in my labors that at times I even skipped food and sleep. Really, it would be no exaggeration to state that the job became my very life, every fiber of the wood I used seemingly linked to my heart and soul.

At last when the chair was completed, I experienced a satisfaction hitherto unknown, for I honestly believed I had achieved a piece of work which immeasurably surpassed all my other creations. As before, I rested the weight of my body on the four legs that supported the chair, first dragging it to a sunny spot on the porch of my workshop. What comfort! What supreme luxury! Not too hard or too soft, the springs seemed to match the cushion with uncanny precision. And as for the leather, what an alluring touch it possessed! This chair not only supported the person who sat in it, but it also seemed to embrace and to hug. Still further, I also noted the perfect reclining angle of the back-support, the delicate puffy swelling of the arm-rests, the perfect symmetry of each of the component parts. Surely, no product could have expressed with greater eloquence the definition of the word "comfort."

I let my body sink deeply into the chair and, caressing the two arm-rests with my hands, gasped with genuine satisfaction and pleasure.

Again my imagination began to play its usual tricks, raising strange fancies in my mind. The scene which I imagined
now rose before my eyes so vividly that, for a moment, I asked
myself if I were not slowly going insane. While in this mental
condition, a weird idea suddenly leaped to my mind. Assuredly,
it was the whispering of the devil himself. Although it was a
sinister idea, it attracted me with a powerful magnetism which
I found impossible to resist.

At first, no doubt, the idea found its seed in my secret yearning to keep the chair for myself. Realizing, however, that this
was totally out of the question, I next longed to accompany
the chair wherever it went. Slowly but steadily, as I continued
to nurse this fantastic notion, my mind fell into the grip of an
almost terrifying temptation. Imagine, Madam, I really and actually made up my mind to carry out that awful scheme to the
end, come what may!

Quickly I took the armchair apart, and then put it together
again to suit my weird purposes. As it was a large armchair,
with the seat covered right down to the level of the floor, and
furthermore, as the back-rest and arm-supports were all large
in dimensions, I soon contrived to make the cavity inside large
enough to accommodate a man without any danger of exposure. Of course, my work was hampered by the large amount
of wooden framework and the springs inside, but with my
usual skill as a craftsman I remodeled the chair so that the
knees could be placed below the seat, the torso and the head
inside the back-rest. Seated thus in the cavity, one could remain perfectly concealed.

As this type of craftsmanship came as second nature to me,
I also added a few finishing touches, such as improved acous-
tics to catch outside noises and of course a peep-hole cut out in
the leather but absolutely unnoticeable. Furthermore, I also
provided storage space for supplies, wherein I placed a few
boxes of hardtack and a water bottle. For another of nature's

needs I also inserted a large rubber bag, and by the time I finished fitting the interior of the chair with these and other unique facilities, it had become quite a habitable place, but not for longer than two or three days at a stretch.

Completing my weird task, I stripped down to my waist and buried myself inside the chair. Just imagine the strange feeling I experienced, Madam! Really, I felt that I had buried myself in a lonely grave. Upon careful reflection I realized that it was indeed a grave. As soon as I entered the chair I was swallowed up by complete darkness, and to everyone else in the world I no longer existed!

Presently a messenger arrived from the dealer's to take delivery of the armchair, bringing with him a large handcart. My apprentice, the only person with whom I lived, was utterly unaware of what had happened. I saw him talking to the messenger.

While my chair was being loaded onto the handcart, one of the cart-pullers exclaimed: "Good God! This chair certainly is heavy! It must weigh a ton!"

When I heard this, my heart leaped to my mouth. However, as the chair itself was obviously an extraordinarily heavy one, no suspicions were aroused, and before long I could feel the vibration of the rattling handcart being pulled along the streets. Of course, I worried incessantly, but at length, that same afternoon, the armchair in which I was concealed was placed with a thud on the floor of a room in the hotel. Later I discovered that it was not an ordinary room, but the lobby.

Now as you may already have guessed long ago, my key motive in this mad venture was to leave my hole in the chair when the coast was clear, loiter around the hotel, and start stealing. Who would dream that a man was concealed inside a chair? Like a fleeting shadow I could ransack every room at will, and by the time any alarm was sounded, I would be safe and sound inside my sanctuary, holding my breath and observing the ridiculous antics of the people outside looking for me.

Possibly you have heard of the hermit crab that is often found on coastal rocks. Shaped like a large spider, this crab crawls about stealthily and, as soon as it hears footsteps, quickly retreats into an empty shell, from which hiding place, with gruesome, hairy front legs partly exposed, it looks furtively about. I was just like this freak monster-crab. But instead of a shell, I had a better shield—a chair which would conceal me far more effectively.

As you can imagine, my plan was so unique and original, so utterly unexpected, that no one was ever the wiser. Consequently, my adventure was a complete success. On the third day after my arrival at the hotel I discovered that I had already taken in quite a haul.

Imagine the thrill and excitement of being able to rob to my heart's content, not to mention the fun I derived from observing the people rushing hither and thither only a few inches away under my very nose, shouting: "The thief went this way!" and: "He went that way!" Unfortunately, I do not have the time to describe all my experiences in detail. Rather, allow me to proceed with my narrative and tell you of a far greater source of weird joy which I managed to discover—in fact, what I am about to relate now is the key point of this letter.

First, however, I must request you to turn your thoughts back to the moment when my chair—and I—were both placed in the lobby of the hotel. As soon as the chair was put on the floor all the various members of the staff took turns testing out the seat. After the novelty wore off they all left the room, and then silence reigned, absolute and complete. However, I could not find the courage to leave my sanctum, for I began to imagine a thousand dangers. For what seemed like ages I kept my ears alerted for the slightest sound. After a while I heard heavy footsteps drawing near, evidently from the direction of the corridor. The next moment the unknown feet must have started to tread on a heavy carpet, for the walking sound died out completely.

Some time later the sound of a man panting, all out of breath, assailed my ears. Before I could anticipate what the next development would be, a large, heavy body like that of a European fell on my knees and seemed to bounce two or three times before settling down. With just a thin layer of leather between the seat of his trousers and my knees, I could almost feel the warmth of his body. As for his broad, muscular shoulders, they rested flatly against my chest, while his two heavy arms were deposited squarely on mine. I could imagine this individual puffing away at his cigar, for the strong aroma came floating to my nostrils.

Just imagine yourself in my queer position, Madam, and reflect for a brief moment on the utterly unnatural state of affairs. As for myself, however, I was utterly frightened, so much so that I crouched in my dark hide-out as if petrified, cold sweat running down my armpits.

Beginning with this individual, several people "sat on my knees" that day, as if they had patiently awaited their turn. No one, however, suspected even for a fleeting moment that the soft "cushion" on which they were sitting was actually human flesh with blood circulating in its veins—confined in a strange world of darkness.

What was it about this mystic hole that fascinated me so? I somehow felt like an animal living in a totally new world. And as for the people who lived in the world outside, I could distinguish them only as people who made weird noises, breathed heavily, talked, rustled their clothes, and possessed soft, round bodies.

Gradually I could begin to distinguish the sitters just by the sense of touch rather than of sight. Those who were fat felt like large jellyfish, while those who were specially thin made me feel that I was supporting a skeleton. Other distinguishing factors consisted of the curve of the spine, the breadth of the shoulder blades, the length of the arms, and the thickness of their thighs as well as the contour of their bottoms. It may seem strange, but I speak nothing but the truth when I say that, although all people may seem alike, there are countless distinguishing traits among all men which can be "seen" merely by the feel of their bodies. In fact, there are just as many differences as in the case of fingerprints or facial contours. This theory, of course, also applies to female bodies.

Usually women are classified in two large categories—the plain and the beautiful. However, in my dark, confined world inside the chair, facial merits or demerits were of secondary importance, being overshadowed by the more meaningful qualities found in the feel of flesh, the sound of the voice, and body odor. (Madam, I do hope you will not be offended by the boldness with which I sometimes speak.)

And so, to continue with my narration, there was one girl—the first who ever sat on me—who kindled in my heart a passionate love. Judging solely by her voice, she was European. At the moment, although there was no one else present in the room, her heart must have been filled with happiness, because she was singing with a sweet voice when she came tripping into the room.

Soon I heard her standing immediately in front of my chair, and without giving any warning she suddenly burst into laughter. The very next moment I could hear her flapping her arms like a fish struggling in a net, and then she sat down—on me! For a period of about thirty minutes she continued to sing, moving her body and feet in tempo with her melody.

For me this was quite an unexpected development, for I had always held aloof from all members of the opposite sex because of my ugly face. Now I realized that I was present in the same room with a European girl whom I had never seen, my skin virtually touching hers through a thin layer of leather.

Unaware of my presence, she continued to act with unreserved freedom, doing as she pleased. Inside the chair, I could visualize myself hugging her, kissing her snowy white neck—if only I could remove that layer of leather. . . .

Following this somewhat unhallowed but nevertheless enjoyable experience, I forgot all about my original intentions of committing robbery. Instead, I seemed to be plunging headlong into a new whirlpool of maddening pleasure.

Long I pondered: "Maybe I was destined to enjoy this type of existence." Gradually the truth seemed to dawn on me. For those who were as ugly and as shunned as myself, it was assuredly wiser to enjoy life inside a chair. For in this strange, dark world I could hear and touch all desirable creatures.

Love in a chair! This may seem altogether too fantastic. Only one who has actually experienced it will be able to vouch for the thrills and the joys it provides. Of course, it is a strange sort of love, limited to the senses of touch, hearing, and smell, a love burning in a world of darkness.

Believe it or not, many of the events that take place in this world are beyond full understanding. In the beginning I had intended only to perpetrate a series of robberies, and then flee. Now, however, I became so attached to my "quarters" that I adjusted them more and more to permanent living.

In my nocturnal prowlings I always took the greatest of precautions, watching each step I took, hardly making a sound. Hence there was little danger of being detected. When I recall, however, that I spent several months inside the chair without being discovered even once, it indeed surprises even me.

For the better part of each day I remained inside the chair, sitting like a contortionist with my arms folded and knees bent. As a consequence I felt as if my whole body was paralyzed.

Furthermore, as I could never stand up straight, my muscles became taut and inflexible, and gradually I began to crawl instead of walk to the washroom. What a madman I was! Even in the face of all these sufferings I could not persuade myself to abandon my folly and leave that weird world of sensuous pleasure.

In the hotel, although there were several guests who stayed for a month or even two, making the place their home, there was always a constant inflow of new guests, and an equal exodus of the old. As a result I could never manage to enjoy a permanent love. Even now, as I bring back to mind all my "love affairs," I can recall nothing but the touch of warm flesh.

Some of the women possessed the firm bodies of ponies; others seemed to have the slimy bodies of snakes; and still others had bodies composed of nothing but fat, giving them the bounce of a rubber ball. There were also the unusual exceptions who seemed to have bodies made only of sheer muscle, like artistic Greek statues. But notwithstanding the species or types, one and all had a special magnetic allure quite distinctive from the others, and I was perpetually shifting the object of my passions.

At one time, for example, an internationally famous dancer came to Japan and happened to stay at this same hotel. Although she sat in my chair only on one single occasion, the contact of her smooth, soft flesh against my own afforded me a hitherto unknown thrill. So divine was the touch of her body that I felt inspired to a state of positive exaltation. On this occasion, instead of my carnal instincts being aroused, I simply felt like a gifted artist being caressed by the magic wand of a fairy.

Strange, eerie episodes followed in rapid succession. However, as space prohibits, I shall refrain from giving a detailed description of each and every case. Instead, I shall continue to outline the general course of events.

One day, several months following my arrival at the hotel, there suddenly occurred an unexpected change in the shape of my destiny. For some reason the foreign proprietor of the hotel was forced to leave for his homeland, and as a result the management was transferred to Japanese hands.

Originating from this change in proprietorship, a new policy was adopted, calling for a drastic retrenchment in expenditures, abolishment of luxurious fittings, and other steps to increase profits through economy. One of the first results of this new policy was that the management put all the extravagant furnishings of the hotel up for auction. Included in the list of items for sale was my chair.

When I learned of this new development, I immediately felt the greatest of disappointments. Soon, however, a voice inside me advised that I should return to the natural world outside— and spend the tidy sum I had acquired by stealing. I, of course, realized that I would no longer have to return to my humble life as a craftsman, for actually I was comparatively wealthy. The thought of my new role in society seemed to overcome my disappointment in having to leave the hotel. Also, when I reflected deeply on all the pleasures which I had derived there, I was forced to admit that, although my "love affairs" had been many, they had all been with foreign women and that somehow something had always been lacking.

I then realized fully and deeply that as a Japanese I really craved a lover of my own kind. While I was turning these thoughts over in my kind, my chair—with me still in it—was sent to a furniture store to be sold at an auction. Maybe this time, I told myself, the chair will be purchased by a Japanese and kept in a Japanese home. With my fingers crossed, I decided to be patient and to continue with my existence in the chair a while longer.

Although I suffered for two or three days in my chair while it stood in front of the furniture store, eventually it came up for sale and was promptly purchased. This, fortunately, was because of the excellent workmanship which had gone into its making, and although it was no longer new, it still had a "dignified bearing."

The purchaser was a high-ranking official who lived in Tokyo. When I was being transferred from the furniture store to the man's palatial residence, the bouncing and vibrating of the vehicle almost killed me. I gritted my teeth and bore up bravely, however, comforted by the thought that at last I had been bought by a Japanese.

Inside his house I was placed in a spacious Western-style study. One thing about the room which gave me the greatest of satisfactions was the fact that my chair was meant more for the use of his young and attractive wife than for his own.

Within a month I had come to be with the wife constantly, united with her as one, so to speak. With the exception of the dining and sleeping hours, her soft body was always seated on my knees for the simple reason that she was engaged in a deep-thinking task.

You have no idea how much I loved this lady! She was the first Japanese woman with whom I had ever come into such close contact, and moreover she possessed a wonderfully appealing body. She seemed the answer to all my prayers! Compared with this, all my other "affairs" with the various women in the hotel seemed like childish flirtations, nothing more.

Proof of the mad love which I now cherished for this intellectual lady was found in the fact that I longed to hold her every moment of the time. When she was away, even for a fleeting moment, I waited for her return like a love-crazed Romeo yearning for his Juliet. Such feelings I had never hitherto experienced.

Gradually I came to want to convey my feelings to her . . . somehow. I tried vainly to carry out my purpose, but always encountered a blank wall, for I was absolutely helpless. Oh, how I longed to have her reciprocate my love! Yes, you may consider this the confession of a madman, for I *was* mad—madly in love with her!

But how could I signal to her? If I revealed myself, the shock of the discovery would immediately prompt her to call her husband and the servants. And that, of course, would be fatal to me, for exposure would not only mean disgrace, but severe punishment for the crimes I had committed.

I therefore decided on another course of action, namely, to add in every way to her comfort and thus awaken in her a natural love for—the chair! As she was a true artist, I somehow felt confident that her natural love of beauty would guide her in the direction I desired. And as for myself, I was willing to find pure contentment in her love even for a material object, for I could find solace in the belief that her delicate feelings of love for even a mere chair were powerful enough to penetrate to the creature that dwelt inside . . . which was myself!

In every way I endeavored to make her more comfortable every time she placed her weight on my chair. Whenever she became tired from sitting long in one position on my humble person, I would slowly move my knees and embrace her more warmly, making her more snug. And when she dozed off to sleep I would move my knees, ever so softly, to rock her into a deeper slumber.

Somehow, possibly by a miracle (or was it just my imagination?), this lady now seemed to love my chair deeply, for every time she sat down she acted like a baby falling into a mother's embrace, or a girl surrendering herself into the arms of her lover. And when she moved herself about in the chair, I felt that she was feeling an almost amorous joy. In this way the fire

of my love and passion rose into a leaping flame that could never be extinguished, and I finally reached a stage where I simply had to make a strange, bold plea.

Ultimately I began to feel that if she would just look at me, even for a brief passing moment, I could die with the deepest contentment.

No doubt, Madam, by this time, you must certainly have guessed who the object of my mad passion is. To put it explicitly, she happens to be none other than yourself, Madam! Ever since your husband brought the chair from that furniture store I have been suffering excruciating pains because of my mad love and longing for you. I am but a worm . . . a loathsome creature.

I have but one request. Could you meet me once, just once? I will ask nothing further of you. I, of course, do not deserve your sympathy, for I have always been nothing but a villain, unworthy even to touch the soles of your feet. But if you will grant me this one request, just out of compassion, my gratitude will be eternal.

Last night I stole out of your residence to write this confession because, even leaving aside the danger, I did not possess the courage to meet you suddenly face to face, without any warning or preparation.

While you are reading this letter, I will be roaming around your house with bated breath. If you will agree to my request, please place your handkerchief on the pot of flowers that stands outside your window. At this signal I will open your front door and enter as a humble visitor. . . .

Thus ended the letter.

Even before Yoshiko had read many pages, some premonition of evil had caused her to become deadly pale. Rising unconsciously, she had fled from the study, from *that chair* upon which she had been seated, and had sought sanctuary in one of the Japanese rooms of her house.

For a moment it had been her intention to stop reading and tear up the eerie message; but somehow, she had read on, with the closely-written sheets laid on a low desk.

Now that she had finished, her premonition was proved correct. That chair on which she had sat from day to day . . . had it really contained a man? If true, what a horrible experience she had unknowingly undergone! A sudden chill came over her, as if ice water had been poured down her back, and the shivers that followed seemed never to stop.

Like one in a trance, she gazed into space. Should she examine the chair? But how could she possibly steel herself for such a horrible ordeal? Even though the chair might now be empty, what about the filthy remains, such as the food and other necessary items which he must have used?

"Madam, a letter for you."

With a start, she looked up and found her maid standing at the doorway with an envelope in her hand.

In a daze, Yoshiko took the envelope and stifled a scream. Horror of horrors! It was another message from the same man! Again her name was written in that same familiar scrawl.

For a long while she hesitated, wondering whether she should open it. At last she mustered up enough courage to break the seal and shakingly took out the pages. This second communication was short and curt, and it contained another breath-taking surprise:

Forgive my boldness in addressing another message to you. To begin with, I merely happen to be one of your ardent admirers. The manuscript which I submitted to you under separate cover was based on pure imagination and my knowledge that you had recently bought *that chair*. It is a sample of my own humble attempts at fictional writing. If you would kindly comment on it, I shall know no greater satisfaction.

For personal reasons I submitted my manuscript prior to writing this letter of explanation, and I assume you have already read it. How did you find it? If, Madam, you have found it amusing or entertaining in some degree, I shall feel that my literary efforts have not been wasted.

Although I purposely refrained from telling you in the manuscript, I intend to give my story the title of "The Human Chair."

> With all my deepest respects
> and sincere wishes, I remain,
> Cordially yours,
>
> . . . .

The Psychological Test

Fukiya might have gone a long way in the world if he had only put his considerable intelligence to better use. Young, bright, and diligent, and the constant pride of his professors at Waseda University in Tokyo—anyone could have seen that he was a man earmarked for a promising future. But, alas, in collaboration with the fates, Fukiya chose to fool all observers. Instead of pursuing a normal scholastic career, he shattered it abruptly by committing . . . *murder!*

Today, many years following his shocking crime, conjecture is still rife as to what strange, unearthly motive actually prompted this gifted young man to carry out his violent plot. Some still persist in their belief that greed for money—the most common of motives—was behind it all. To some extent, this explanation is plausible, for it is true that young Fukiya, who was working his way through school, was keenly feeling the leanness of his purse. Also, being the intellectual that he was, his pride may have been so deeply wounded at having to consume so much of his precious time working that he might have felt that crime was the only way out. But are these altogether obvious reasons sufficient to explain away the almost

[Certain British spellings have been amended. Ed.]

unparalleled viciousness of the crime he committed? Others have advanced the far more likely theory that Fukiya was a born criminal and had committed the crime merely for its own sake. At any rate, whatever his hidden motives, it is an undeniable fact that Fukiya, like many other intellectual criminals before him, had set out to commit the perfect crime.

From the day Fukiya began his first classes at Waseda he was restless and uneasy. Some noxious force seemed to be eating away at his mind, coaxing him, goading him on to execute a "plot" which was still only a vague outline in his mind—like a shadow in a mist. Day in and day out, while attending lectures, chatting with his friends on the campus, or working at odd jobs to cover his expenses, he kept puzzling over what was making him so nervous. And then, one day, he became specially chummy with a classmate named Saito, and his "plot" began to take definite shape.

Saito was a quiet student of about the same age as Fukiya, and likewise hard up for money. For nearly a year now he had rented a room in the home of a widow who had been left in quite comfortable circumstances upon the death of her husband, a government official. Nearly sixty years old, the woman was extremely avaricious and stingy. Despite the fact that the income from rent on several houses ensured her a comfortable living, she still greedily added to her wealth by lending money in small sums to reliable acquaintances. But, then, she was childless, and as a result had gradually come to regard money, ever since the early stages of her widowhood, as a substitute consolation. In the case of Saito, however, she had taken him as a lodger more for protection than for gain: like all people who hoard money, she kept a large sum cached away in her house.

Fukiya had no sooner learned all this from his friend Saito than he was tempted by the widow's money. "What earthly good will it ever do her anyway?" he asked himself repeatedly, following two or three visits to the house. "Anyone can see that the withered old hag is not long for this world. But look at me! I'm young, full of life and ambition, with a bright future to look forward to."

His thoughts constantly revolved about this subject, leading to but one conclusion: *He just had to have that money!* But how to get it? The answer to this question grew into the web of a horrible plan. First, however, Fukiya decided that all successful plots depended on one important factor—skillful and thorough preparation. So, in a subtle and casual manner, he set about the task of getting as much information as possible from his schoolmate Saito about the old woman and her hidden money.

One day Saito casually made a remark which nearly bowled Fukiya over, for it was the very information he had long been yearning to know.

"You know, Fukiya," Saito remarked laughingly, utterly unsuspecting the foul plot that was being nursed in his friend's mind, "the old woman surely is crazy about her money. Nearly every month she thinks up a new place to hide it. Today, quite by accident, I came across her latest 'safety deposit vault,' and I must say she's exceedingly original. Can you guess where it is?"

Suppressing his excitement with an actor's finesse, Fukiya yawned and blandly remarked: "I'm afraid I couldn't even make a guess."

Saito was easily caught in the artful trap. "Well, then, I'll tell you," he quickly said, somewhat disappointed by the other's lack of interest. "As you probably know, when a person tries to hide money he usually puts it under the floor or in some secret cavity or hole in the wall. But my dear landlady's far more ingenious. Do you remember that dwarf pine-tree that sits in the alcove of the guest room? Well, that's the newest place she's chosen to hide her money—right inside the earth in the pot. Don't you think she's awfully clever? No thief would ever think of looking in a place like that."

As the days passed, Saito appeared to have forgotten the conversation, but not Fukiya. Having devoured Saito's every word, he was now determined to take possession of the old woman's money. But there were still certain details which had to be figured out before he could make his first move. One of these was the all-important problem of how to divert even the faintest suspicion from himself. Other questions, such as remorse and the attendant pangs of conscience, troubled him not in the least. All this talk of Raskolnikov, in Dostoyevsky's *Crime and Punishment*, crucified by the unseen terrors of a haunted heart was, to Fukiya, sheer nonsense. After all, he reasoned, everything depended on one's point of view. Was Napoleon to be condemned as a mass murderer because he had been responsible for the deaths of so many people? Certainly not. In fact, he rather admired the ex-corporal who had risen to be an emperor, no matter what the means.

Now definitely committed to the deed, Fukiya calmly awaited his chance. As he called frequently to see Saito, he already knew the general lay-out of the house, and a few more visits provided him with all the details he needed. For example, he soon learned that the old woman rarely went out of doors. This was a disappointment. Day after day she remained seated in her private parlor in one wing of the house in absolute silence. If, however, sheer necessity did coax her to leave the comfort of her shell, she would first post her maidservant, a simple country girl, as a "sentry" to keep watch over the house. Fukiya soon came to realize that in the face of these circumstances his contemplated adventure in crime would be no easy matter. On the contrary, if he was ever to succeed, he would have to use his greatest cunning.

For a full month Fukiya considered various schemes, but one by one he discarded them all as faulty. Finally, after wracking his brain to the point of exhaustion, Fukiya came to the conclusion that there was but one solution: *He must murder the old woman!* He also reasoned that the old woman's hidden fortune would certainly be large enough to justify killing her and reminded himself that the most notorious burglars in history had always eliminated their victims on the sound theory that "the dead tell no tales."

Carefully, Fukiya began to map out the safest course of action. This took time, but through the innocent Saito he knew that the hiding place had not been changed, and he felt he could afford to make each tiny detail perfect, even down to the most trivial matter.

One day, quite unexpectedly, Fukiya realized that his long-awaited moment had arrived. First, he heard that Saito would be absent from the house all day on school business. The maid-servant, too, would be away on an errand, not to return until evening. Quite by coincidence, just two days previously Fukiya had gone to the trouble of verifying that the money was still concealed in the pot of the dwarf pine. He had ascertained this quite easily. While visiting Saito he had casually gone into the old landlady's room "to pay his respects" and during the course of his conversation had ingeniously let drop a remark here and there referring to her hidden cache of money. An artful student of psychology, he had watched the old woman's eyes whenever he mentioned the words *hiding place*. As he had anticipated, her eyes turned unintentionally toward the potted tree in the alcove every time.

On the day of the murder Fukiya dressed in his usual school uniform and cap, plus his black student's cloak. He also wore gloves to be sure he would leave no fingerprints. Long ago he had decided against a disguise, for he had realized that masquerade outfits would be easy to trace. He was of the firm conviction that the simpler and more open his crime was, the harder it would be to detect. In his pockets he carried a longish but ordinary jackknife and a large purse. He had purchased these commonplace objects at a small general-merchandise store at a time when it was full of customers, and he had paid the price asked without haggling. So he was confident no one would remember him as the purchaser.

Immersed in his thoughts, Fukiya slowly walked toward the scene of his contemplated crime. As he gradually drew near the neighborhood he reminded himself for about the tenth time that it was essential for him *not* to be observed entering the house. But supposing he accidentally ran into an acquaintance before he could reach his victim's gate? Well, this would not be serious, so long as the acquaintance could be persuaded to believe that he was only out taking a stroll, as was his custom.

Fifteen minutes later he arrived in front of the old woman's house. Although he had fortunately not met a soul who knew him, he found his breath coming in short gasps. This, to him, was a nasty sensation. Somehow he was beginning to feel more and more like an ordinary thief and prowler than the suave and nonchalant prince of crime he had always pictured himself to be.

Fighting to control his nerves, Fukiya furtively looked about in all directions. Finally, satisfied that he was still unobserved, he turned his attention to the house itself. This was sandwiched in between two other houses, but conveniently isolated from them by two rows of trees on both sides, thick with foliage and forming natural fences. Facing the house on the opposite side there stood a long concrete wall which encircled a wealthy estate occupying a complete block.

Slowly and noiselessly, he opened the gate, holding the tiny bell which was attached, so as to prevent it from tinkling. Once inside the yard, he walked stealthily to one of the side entrances and called out softly.

"Good morning," he called, noting with alarm that his voice did not sound at all like his own.

Immediately there was a reply, accompanied by the rustling sound of a kimono, and the next moment the old woman came to the door.

"Good morning, Mr. Fukiya," she greeted, kneeling and bowing politely. "I'm afraid your friend Mr. Saito isn't in."

"It's—it's you I wish to speak to," Fukiya explained quickly, "although the matter concerns Saito."

"Then please come in," she invited.

After he had taken off his shoes, she ushered him into the reception room, where she apologized for being alone in the house. "My maid is out today," she said, "so you must excuse me while I get the tea things. I won't be a minute." She rose and turned to leave the room.

This was the very opportunity Fukiya was waiting for. As the old woman bent herself a little in order to open the paper door, he pounced on her from behind and slowly proceeded to strangle her with his two gloved hands. Feebly, the old woman struggled, and one of her fingers scratched a folded screen which was standing close by.

After the old woman went limp, Fukiya carefully examined the damage. The screen had two folds and its surface was covered with gold flakes and a painting showing Komachi, a noted beauty of the feudal era. It was precisely on Komachi's face that the old woman had scratched in her death throes.

Fukiya soon recovered his composure, for he felt that this was too trivial to mean anything. He put the matter out of his mind and, going to the alcove, grabbed the pine tree by the trunk and pulled it out of the pot. As he had expected, he found a bundle lying in the base of the pot neatly wrapped up in oil-paper. Eagerly he undid the wrapping and grinned with satisfaction when a thick wad of paper money came to light.

Wasting no time, Fukiya took *half* of the money, stuffed it into the new purse that he took out of his pocket, re-wrapped the rest in the same oilpaper, and replaced the package at the bottom of the pot. He considered this move to be his master stroke, for he felt certain that it would throw the police miles off the track. Considering that the old woman was the only person who could have known exactly how much money she had hidden, no one would be any the wiser even if the amount were reduced to one half of the original sum.

Fukiya's next move was to stab the old woman carefully in the heart with the long jackknife. Then he wiped the blade on the woman's kimono and replaced it in his pocket. The purpose of this strange act was simply to make doubly sure that she could not be revived, a possibility he had often read about in crime novels. He had not killed her with the knife, for fear her blood might spatter on his clothing.

Fukiya replaced the tree in the pot, smoothed out the earth, and otherwise made certain that no clues had been left behind. Then he went out of the room. After closing the door, he tiptoed silently to the side entrance. Here, as he tied his shoelaces, he wondered if his shoes might leave tell-tale marks. But then he decided there was no danger, for the entryway was floored with cement. Stepping out into the garden, he felt even more secure, because it was a sunny day and the ground was hard and dry. Now, the only thing left for him to do was to walk to the front gate, open it, and vanish from the scene.

His heart was beating wildly, for he realized that one slip now would be fatal. He strained his ears for the slightest warning of danger, such as approaching footfalls, but all he could hear were the melodious notes of a Japanese harp tinkling in the distance. Straightening his shoulders, Fukiya strode to the gate, opened it boldly, and walked away.

Four or five blocks away from the old woman's house there stood a high, stone wall enclosing an old Shinto shrine. Fukiya dropped his jackknife and his blood-spattered gloves through a crevice in the wall down into a ditch, then walked on in a

leisurely manner to a small park where he frequently went walking. Here he sat on a bench and casually watched several children playing on the swings.

After spending considerable time in the park, he rose from his seat, yawned and stretched, and then made his way to a nearby police station. Greeting the sergeant at the desk with a perfectly innocent look, he produced his well-filled purse.

"Officer, I just found this purse on the street. It's full of money, so I thought I'd better turn it in."

The policeman took the purse, examined its contents, and asked several routine questions. Fukiya, perfectly calm and self-possessed, answered straightforwardly, indicating the place and time he had made his "find." Naturally, all the information he gave was pure fabrication, with one exception: he gave his correct name and address.

After filling out several forms, the sergeant handed him a receipt. Fukiya pocketed the receipt, and for a moment wondered again if he was acting wisely. From every point of view, however, this was assuredly the safest course to take. Nobody knew that the old lady's money had been reduced by half. Also, it was quite obvious to Fukiya that no one would come to claim the purse. According to Japanese law, all the money in the purse would become his if no one claimed it within one year. Of course, it would be a long time to wait, but what of it? It was just like money in the bank—something he could count on, something to look forward to.

On the other hand, if he had hidden the money, to await an opportune time to spend it, it would have meant risking his neck every moment of the day. But the way he had chosen eliminated even the remotest danger of detection, even if the old lady had kept a record of the serial numbers of the banknotes.

While walking home from the police station Fukiya continued to gloat silently over the masterful way he had carried out his crime. "A simple case of sheer genius," he said to himself with a chuckle. "And what a big joke on the police. Imagine! A thief turning in his spoils! Under such circumstances, how could anyone possibly suspect me? Why, not even the Great Buddha himself would ever guess the truth!"

On the following day, after waking from a sound and untroubled sleep, Fukiya looked at the morning paper, delivered to his bedside by the maid of the boardinghouse. Stifling a yawn, he glanced at the page which carried the human-interest stories. Suddenly he caught sight of a brief item which caused his eyes to open wide. The first part of the story was an account of the discovery of the old woman's body. This was neither surprising nor startling to Fukiya. But the report went on to disclose that his friend Saito had been arrested by the police as the main suspect, having been discovered with a large sum of money on his person.

Actually, Fukiya thought, this fact too was nothing to become disturbed about. Instead, the development was decidedly advantageous to his own security. As one of Saito's closest friends, however, he also realized that he would have to inquire about him at the police station.

Fukiya dressed hastily and then called at the police station mentioned in the newspaper story. This turned out to be the very same place where he had reported the "finding" of the purse. "Curse my luck!" he swore to himself when he made this embarrassing discovery. Why hadn't he selected a different police station to report the money to? Well, it was too late now to change things.

Skillfully, he expressed deep anxiety over the unfortunate plight of his friend. He asked if they would permit him to see Saito and received a polite no. He then tried to make a few inquiries into the circumstances which had led to his friend's arrest, but here again he was refused.

Fukiya, however, didn't much care, for even without being told he could easily imagine what had happened. On the fateful day, Saito must have returned to the house ahead of the maid. By that time, of course, he himself had already committed his horrible deed and left the house. Then Saito must have found the corpse. Before reporting the crime to the police, however, he must have remembered the money hidden in the pot. If this was the work of a robber, Saito must have figured, the money would surely be gone. Curious to know if his reasoning was correct, he had examined the pot and had found the money there wrapped in oilpaper. And Fukiya could easily imagine what must have happened after that.

Undoubtedly Saito was tempted to keep the money for himself. This was a natural reaction, although, of course, it was a foolish thing for him to do. Thinking that everybody would believe that the murderer of the old woman had stolen the money, Saito pocketed the whole amount. And his next move? This, too, was easy to surmise. He had recklessly gone ahead and reported his discovery of the old woman's corpse, with the money still on his person, never suspecting that he would be one of the first to be questioned and searched. What an utter fool!

But wait, Fukiya reasoned further, Saito would certainly put up a desperate struggle to clear himself of suspicion. Then what? Would his statements possibly incriminate him, Fukiya, in any way? If Saito just kept insisting that the money was his, all might be well. But, then, the fact that the amount was exceptionally large—much too large for a student like Saito to possess—might give the lie to such a statement. The only alternative left for Saito would be to tell the truth—the whole truth. This would lead, by clever cross-examination on the part of the prosecutor, to the revelation that Saito had also told Fukiya where the old lady had hidden her money.

"Only two days preceding the day of the crime," Fukiya could even hear Saito telling the court, "my friend Fukiya conversed with the victim in the very room in which she was murdered. Knowing that she had that money hidden in the tree pot, could he not have committed the crime? I also wish to remind you, gentlemen of the court, that Fukiya has always been notorious for being financially hard up!"

Although feeling decidedly uncomfortable after this soliloquy, Fukiya's optimism soon conquered his initial dismay. Emerging from the police station with a perfectly blank look on his face, he returned to his boardinghouse and ate a rather late breakfast. While eating, his original bravado returned, and he even made a point of telling the maid who served him about several aspects of the case.

Shortly after, he went to school, where he found, both on the campus and in the classrooms, that Saito's arrest as a suspect in the murder case was the main topic of conversation.

The investigator placed in charge of this sensational case was District Attorney Kasamori, noted not only as a man with excellent legal training, but also well known for valuable accomplishments of his own, especially in the field of psychological research. Whenever he came across a case which could not be unraveled by the standard methods of crime detection, he employed his fund of psychological knowledge with amazing results. With a man of Kasamori's reputation taking in hand the case of the old lady's murder, the public immediately became convinced that the mystery would soon be solved.

Kasamori too was confident that he could ultimately crack the case, no matter how complex it appeared at this early stage of the investigation. He began with a preliminary check of everything connected with the case, so that by the time it reached a public trial every single phase would be as clear as daylight. As the investigation proceeded, however, he found the case more and more difficult to handle. From the outset, the police kept insisting that no one but Saito could be the guilty party. Kasamori himself admitted the logic of the police theory, for, after all, every person who had been even remotely connected with the murdered old woman had been investigated and cleared of suspicion—every one, that is, except her student lodger, the hapless Saito. Fukiya too had been among those who had been questioned, along with creditors of the old woman, her tenants, and even casual acquaintances, but he had quickly been eliminated.

In the case of Saito, there was one major point which worked to his great disadvantage. This was that he was extremely weak by nature and, completely terrorized by the stern atmosphere of the court, he was unable to answer even the simplest questions without first stuttering and stammering and showing all the symptoms of a man with a guilty conscience. Furthermore, in his excited state, he often retracted his previous statements, forgot vital details, and then tried to cover up by making other contradictory remarks, all of which tended only to incriminate him further and further. Simultaneously, there was another factor which tortured him and drove him to the verge of insanity. This was the fact that he *was* guilty of having stolen half of the old woman's money, precisely as Fukiya had theorized.

The district attorney carefully summed up the evidence, circumstantial as it was, against Saito, and pitied him deeply. It could not be denied that all the odds were against him. But, Kasamori asked himself again and again, had this weak, blubbering fool been capable of committing such a vicious, cold-blooded murder? He doubted it. So far Saito had not confessed, and conclusive proof of his guilt was still lacking.

A month went by, but the preliminary probe had not yet been completed. The district attorney became decidedly annoyed and impatient at the slow pace of the investigation.

"Curse the slow-grinding wheels of the law!" he exploded to a subordinate one day, while rechecking his documents on the case for what was probably the hundredth time. "At this rate, it'll take us a thousand years to solve the case." He then strode angrily to another desk and picked up a sheaf of routine documents filled out by the captain of the police station in whose jurisdiction the murder of the old lady fell. He looked casually at one of the papers and noticed that a purse containing ninety-five thousand yen in thousand-yen notes had been found at a spot near the old lady's house on the same day of the murder. The finder of the money, he further learned from the report, was a student, Fukiya by name, and a close friend of Saito's, the key murder suspect! For some reason—possibly because of the urgency of other duties—the police captain had failed to submit his report earlier.

After finishing reading the report, Kasamori's eyes lit up with a strange glow. For a full month now he had felt like a person fumbling in the dark. And then came this information, like a thin ray of light. Could it have any significance, any bearing on the case at hand? He decided to find out without delay.

Fukiya was quickly summoned, and the district attorney questioned him closely. After a full hour's questioning, however, Kasamori found he was getting nowhere. Asked as to why he had not mentioned the incident of his finding the purse when he had been interrogated previously in connection with the murder, Fukiya maintained calmly that he had not thought the matter to have any bearing on the case.

This reply, given straightforwardly, sounded most reasonable, for the money believed to have belonged to the old lady had been found in Saito's possession. Naturally, therefore, who could have imagined that the money found on the street was also a part of the old lady's property?

Nevertheless, Kasamori was deeply puzzled. Was it nothing but a mere coincidence that the very man who was a close friend of Saito's, the leading suspect, the man who, according to Saito's testimony in court, had also known where the old lady had hidden her money, had picked up so large a sum at a spot not far from the place where the murder had been committed? Here, indeed, was a conundrum worthy of the mind of a master sleuth.

Struggling angrily with the problem, the district attorney cursed the unfortunate fact that the serial numbers of the banknotes had not been recorded by the old woman. Had they been recorded, it would have been a most simple task to verify whether the money found by Fukiya was part of the same loot.

"If only I could find one single clue," he kept repeating to himself.

In the days that followed, Kasamori revisited the scene of the crime and talked to the victim's relatives, going over the same ground again and again, but all to no avail. He had to admit that he was up against a wall, with not a single tangible clue to follow up.

So far as he could see, the only possible way in which he could explain the episode of Fukiya's finding the purse was that the man had stolen half of the old lady's savings, left the remainder in the hiding place, put the stolen money in a purse, and pretended that he had found it on the street. But was it really possible that such a fantastic thing could have been done? The purse, of course, had been subjected to the closest scrutiny and placed under a microscope for even the faintest of possible clues, but all these efforts had proved negative. Also, according to Fukiya's own statement, he had taken a walk on the day of the murder; in fact, he had even admitted that he had passed the old lady's house. Would a man who was guilty be so bold as to make such a dangerous admission? And then, what about the weapon which had been used to stab the old woman? The entire house and garden as well as the surrounding area within a large radius had been searched with a fine-tooth comb, but there was not a trace of it.

In the absence of conclusive evidence to the contrary, Kasamori felt that the police were justified in pointing to Saito as the most likely suspect. But then again, the district attorney reasoned, if Saito could be guilty, so could Fukiya! Thus, after an investigation which had stretched out to a full month and a half, the only point which had been established was that there were two possible suspects, but without a shred of concrete evidence to convict either.

Reaching this impasse, Kasamori decided there was still one other method he could use in his attempt to break the case. This was to subject the two suspects to a psychological test—a method which had been useful in the past.

When he had first been questioned by the police, two or three days after the murder, Fukiya had learned that the district attorney who had been put in charge of the case was the noted amateur psychologist Kasamori, and the information filled him with panic. Cool and collected as he had been until then, he soon came to dread the very sound of the district attorney's name, especially after he had been summoned a second time and questioned by Kasamori himself. Supposing, just supposing, he were to be subjected to a psychological test. What then? Would he be able to hold his own in the face of such an experiment, the nature of which he knew absolutely nothing about?

The shock of this possibility was so stunning that he became too uneasy to attend his classes. He remained in his room, on the pretext of illness, and tried desperately to figure out how he could match wits for wits. Of course, there was absolutely no way of anticipating the form of psychological test that Kasamori might employ. Fukiya, therefore, applied all the test methods he could possibly imagine on himself in order to discover the best possible way to circumvent them. Since a psychological test, by nature, was a method applied to reveal all false statements, Fukiya's first thought was that it would be utterly impossible to lie his way out of such a test.

Fukiya knew there were psychological tests which used lie-detector devices to record physical reactions. He had also heard that there was a simpler method which used a stopwatch to measure the time it took a suspect to answer questions. Reflecting upon the many and various psychological methods of crime detection, Fukiya became more and more concerned. Supposing he were caught by a surprise question like "You're the one who killed the old woman, aren't you?" fired at him point-blank? Fukiya felt confident that he would be able to shoot back calmly: "What proof do you have for such a wild supposition?" But if a lie detector were to be used, wouldn't it record his startled state of mind? Wouldn't it be absolutely impossible for a normal human being to prevent such physical reactions?

Fukiya tried asking himself various hypothetical questions. Strangely, no matter how unexpected his questions were, when they were addressed *to himself by himself*, he could not imagine that they produced any physical changes within him. Gradually he became convinced that so long as he avoided becoming nervously excited, he would be safe even in the face of the most accurate instrument.

While conducting these various experiments on himself, Fukiya suddenly became convinced that the effects of a psychological test might be neutralized by training. He became sure that the reaction of a man's nerves to a pointed question would become less each time the question was repeated. Granting that his reasoning was sound, Fukiya told himself, the best method of neutralization was to become accustomed to the questions. He reasoned that his own questions to himself produced no reaction because he already knew both question and answer before he spoke.

Fukiya painstakingly began to examine every page of a thick dictionary and to jot down those words which might possibly be used in questions to be thrown at him. For a full week he spent most of his waking hours this way, training his nerves against all possible questions. Then, feeling that his mind had been fairly well fortified in this field, he turned to another. This was the word-association test, which Fukiya knew psychiatrists used widely in examining patients.

As Fukiya understood it, the patient—or accused—would be told to answer any word given him with the first word that came to his mind, and then the examiner would call off a list of words with absolutely no bearing on the case—"screen," "desk," "ink," "pen," and the like. The significance of the test lay in the fact that the word given in reply would have some mental association with the previously recited word. For example, if the word happened to be "screen," the culprit might come out with such words as "window," "window sill," "paper," or "door." And in the course of the test such incriminating words as "knife," "money," or "purse" would be slipped in so as to befuddle the accused in his association of ideas.

In Fukiya's case, for instance, if he were not on his guard, he might reply "money" to "dwarf tree," thereby unconsciously admitting that he knew money to have been stolen from the pot of the tree. On the other hand, if he prepared for the ordeal in advance, he could answer with a harmless word like "earthernware" instead of "money." Then, of course, he would be in the clear.

Fukiya knew that, in conducting the "word diagnosis," the exact time elapsing between question and answer was always recorded. If, for example, the accused said "door" in reply to "screen" in one second and then took three seconds to say "earthernware" in reply to "dwarf tree," it could be inferred that the man had taken more time to frame the second reply in order to suppress the first idea which leaped to his mind. Such a time discrepancy, of course, would arouse suspicion.

Fukiya also reasoned that if he were given a word test, it would be far safer to answer in the most obviously natural manner. He, therefore, decided that in reply to "dwarf tree" he would say either "pine" or "money" because, even if he had not been the culprit, the police would know that he would be sufficiently acquainted with the facts of the crime for this to be a natural answer for him to give. One question, however, called for deeper thought. This was the matter of timing. But he felt that this too could be managed by careful training. The important thing was that if a word like "dwarf tree" was fired at him, he should be able to reply "money" or "pine" without a moment's hesitation.

For several days Fukiya worked hard at training himself, until finally he felt that he could satisfactorily pass the strictest test. Furthermore, he derived immense consolation from the knowledge that Saito, although innocent of the murder, would also be exposed to the same volley of questions, and would certainly exhibit a similar degree of nervousness.

The more Fukiya considered all these possibilities, the greater became his sense of security and self-confidence. In fact, now that he was once again feeling completely at ease, he was able to whistle and sing, and even to wish strongly for a summons from District Attorney Kasamori.

It was the day after the district attorney had subjected both suspects to psychological tests, and Kasamori was in his study at home, busily going over the results of the tests. Suddenly his maid announced that he had a visitor.

Literally buried under his papers, the district attorney was in no mood to play host, so he growled impatiently to his servant: "Kindly tell whoever it is that I'm too busy to see anyone today."

"Yes, sir," the maid replied obediently, but as she turned, the door suddenly opened, and the caller popped his head in playfully.

"Good afternoon, Mr. District Attorney," the caller said cheerfully, ignoring the startled look of the servant. "Don't tell me you're too busy even to see your old friend Akechi."

Kasamori dropped his pince-nez and looked up sharply. But immediately his face broadened into a happy grin.

"Why, hello, Dr. Akechi," he replied. "I didn't know it was you. Forgive me. Step right in and make yourself comfortable. As a matter of fact, I was hoping you'd drop in."

Kasamori dismissed the maid with a grunt and motioned to his guest to be seated. A sleuth with a mind keen as a razor and a unique technique for solving knotty problems, Dr. Kogoro Akechi was the one man whom the district attorney would have stopped to talk to even if he had been on his way to catch a train. On several previous occasions he had asked for Dr. Akechi's cooperation in cracking what had been labeled "impossible cases," and in every instance the man had lived up to his reputation as one of Japan's most remarkable detectives.

After lighting a cigarette, Dr. Akechi nodded meaningfully toward the stacks of papers on the district attorney's desk.

"I see you're very busy," he remarked casually. "Is it the case of the old woman who was murdered recently?"

"Yes," the district attorney replied. "Frankly, I'm at the end of my rope."

"Pessimism doesn't become you, Mr. District Attorney," said Dr. Akechi with a dry laugh. "Come, now, tell me the results of the psychological tests you gave your two suspects."

Kasamori raised his eyebrows. "How the devil did you know about my tests?" he asked sharply.

"One of your assistants told me," Dr. Akechi explained. "You see, I'm deeply interested in the case too, so I thought I'd come and offer you my humble services."

"It was kind of you to come," Kasamori replied gratefully and quickly launched into a discussion of his complicated experiments.

"The results, as you will notice," he said, "are clear enough, but there is something that has me completely baffled. Yesterday I gave each suspect two tests, a lie-detector test based on

71

pulse measurements and a word-association test. In Fukiya's case the pulse measurements were almost always above suspicion. But when I compared the results of the word-association test, I found a tremendous difference between Saito and Fukiya. In fact, the results were so far apart that I must admit I'm completely at a loss for an explanation. Just look at this questionnaire and observe the differences in the time taken by the two suspects in their replies to the same words."

Kasamori then handed Dr. Akechi the following tabulation of the results of the word-association test:

WORD GIVEN	FUKIYA		SAITO	
	Answer	Time Taken	Answer	Time Taken
head	hair	0.9 sec.	tail	1.2 sec.
green	grass	0.7 "	grass	1.1 "
water	hot water	0.9 "	fish	1.3 "
sing	songs	1.1 "	geisha	1.5 "
long	short	1.0 "	cord	1.2 "
* kill	knife	0.8 "	crime	3.1 "
boat	river	0.9 "	water	2.2 "
window	door	0.8 "	glass	1.5 "
food	beefsteak	1.0 "	fish	1.3 "
* money	bank notes	0.7 "	bank	3.5 "
cold	water	1.1 "	winter	3.2 "
illness	cold	1.6 "	tuberculosis	2.3 "
needle	thread	1.0 "	thread	1.2 "
* pine	dwarf tree	0.8 "	tree	2.3 "
mountain	high	0.9 "	river	1.4 "
* blood	flowing	1.0 "	red	3.9 "
new	old	0.8 "	dress	3.0 "
hate	spider	1.2 "	sickness	1.5 "
* dwarf tree	pine	0.6 "	flower	6.2 "

Continued from facing page

WORD GIVEN	FUKIYA		SAITO	
	Answer	Time Taken	Answer	Time Taken
bird	flying	0.9 sec.	canary	3.6 sec.
book	library	1.0 "	novel	1.3 "
* oilpaper	conceal	1.0 "	parcel	4.0 "
friend	Saito	1.1 "	Fukiya	1.8 "
box	wood	1.0 "	doll	1.2 "
* crime	murder	0.7 "	police	3.7 "
woman	lover	1.0 "	sister	1.3 "
painting	screen	0.9 "	landscape	1.3 "
* steal	money	0.7 "	necklace	4.1 "
Note: words marked with an asterisk (*) are directly related to the crime.				

"You see, everything is very plain," said the district attorney after Dr. Akechi had examined the paper. "According to this, Saito must have willfully resorted to trickery. This is evident from the fact that he took so much time to respond, not only to the incriminating words, but also to the unimportant dummy words. Also, the long time he took in replying to 'dwarf tree' probably indicates he was trying to suppress such natural, but in his opinion incriminating, words as 'money' or 'pine.' Now, on the other hand, take the case of Fukiya. He said 'pine' in reply to 'dwarf tree,' 'conceal' in reply to 'oilpaper,' and 'murder' in reply to 'crime.' Surely, if he were really guilty, he would have avoided uttering those words. Yet he replied in a perfectly matter-of-fact tone, without the slightest hesitation. From these facts, therefore, I am strongly inclined to rule him out as a suspect. At the same time, however, when it comes to deciding positively that Saito is the guilty man, I simply can't bring myself to it, despite this record."

Dr. Akechi listened calmly to the district attorney's reasoning without making any effort to interrupt. But after the latter had concluded his summing up, Dr. Akechi's eyes gleamed brightly, and he began to speak.

"Have you ever stopped to consider the weak points of a psychological test?" he began. "De Quires has stated, in criticism of the views entertained by Muensterberg, who advocated the psychological test, that although the system was devised as a substitute for torture, its actual result might well incriminate the innocent just as much as had trial by torture, thus allowing the real criminal to escape. Muensterberg himself has stated in his books that a psychological test is definitely effective in verifying whether a suspected person knows a certain other person, or place, or thing, but that for other purposes it is very dangerous. I realize that my telling you all this, Kasamori, is decidedly superfluous, but I just wanted to call your attention to these vital facts."

The district attorney replied, with a trace of annoyance in his voice, that he was aware of these facts.

"Well, then," Dr. Akechi continued, "let us study the case at hand from an entirely different angle. Supposing—just supposing—an innocent man who is extremely nervous is suspected of a crime. He is arrested at the scene of the crime and is, therefore, aware of all the circumstances and the macabre setting. In such an event could he preserve his composure if he was subjected to a rigid psychological test? He might very naturally say to himself: 'They are going to test me. What shall I say to escape suspicion?' Considering that his mind would naturally be greatly excited, would not a psychological test conducted under such circumstances tend to incriminate the innocent party, as De Quiros has mentioned?"

"I suppose you are talking about Saito," said the district attorney, still annoyed.

"Yes," Dr. Akechi replied. "And now, granting that my reasoning is sound, he would be entirely innocent of the murder, although of course, the possibility still remains that he might actually have stolen the money. And now comes the big question: Who killed the old woman?"

Kasamori interrupted abruptly at this point. "Come now, Dr. Akechi," he said impatiently. "Don't keep me in suspense. Have you come to any definite conclusion as to who the actual killer is?"

"Yes, I think so," Dr. Akechi replied, smiling broadly. "Judging by the results of your psychological tests, I believe Fukiya is our man, although, of course, I cannot swear to it yet. Could we have him brought here? If I can ask him a few more questions, I feel positive that I can get to the bottom of this most intriguing case."

"But what about evidence?" the district attorney asked, taken aback by the other's cool manner. "Just *how* are you going to get your proof?"

"Give a guilty man enough rope," rejoined Dr. Akechi philosophically, "and he'll supply enough evidence to hang himself."

Dr. Akechi then outlined his theory in detail. After hearing it, Kasamori clapped his hands to call his servant. Then, taking up pen and paper from his desk, he wrote the following note, addressed to Fukiya:

Your friend Saito has been found guilty of the crime. As there are a few points I wish to discuss with you, I request you to call at my private residence immediately.

He signed the message and handed it to the servant.

Fukiya had just returned from school when he received the note. Unaware that it was the bait for a carefully laid trap, he was elated over the news. Without bothering even to have his supper, he hurried to the district attorney's house.

As soon as Fukiya entered the study, District Attorney Kasamori greeted him warmly and invited him to sit down.

"I owe you an apology, Mr. Fukiya," he said, "for having suspected you for so long. Now that I know you to be innocent,

I thought you might like to hear a few of the circumstances surrounding your complete exoneration."

The district attorney ordered refreshments for everybody and then ceremoniously introduced the student to Dr. Akechi, although he used quite a different name for the latter.

"Mr. Yamamoto," he explained, indicating Dr. Akechi without batting an eyelash, "is a lawyer who has been appointed by the old woman's heirs to settle her estate."

After refreshments of tea and rice-cakes, they discussed various unimportant matters, Fukiya talking very freely. In fact, as the time quickly sped by, he became the most loquacious of the three. Suddenly, however, he glanced at his wrist watch and rose abruptly.

"I didn't realize that it was so late," he announced apologetically. "If you'll forgive me, I think I'd better be leaving."

"Of course, of course," said the district attorney drily.

Dr. Akechi, however, suddenly interrupted. "One moment, please," he said to Fukiya. "There is just one trivial question I'd like to ask you before you leave. I wonder if you know there was a two-fold gold screen standing in the room where the old woman was murdered? It has been slightly damaged, and a minor legal issue has been raised over it. You see, it appears that the screen didn't belong to the old woman, but was being held by her as security for a loan. And now the owner has come forward with the demand that he be reimbursed for the damage. My clients, however, are reluctant to agree to this, for they contend that the screen might have been damaged *before* it was brought into the house. Really, of course, it's a very trivial matter, but if you could by any chance help me to clear it up, I would be more than grateful. The reason I'm asking is because I understand you frequently visited the house to see your friend Saito. Perhaps you may have noticed the screen. Saito, of course, was asked about it, but in his excited condition nothing that he said seemed to make much sense. I also tried to contact the old lady's maid, but she's already returned to her home in the country, and I haven't yet had an opportunity to write to her."

Although Dr. Akechi had mentioned all this in a perfectly matter-of-fact tone of voice, Fukiya felt a slight tremor in his heart. But he quickly reassured himself: "Why should I be startled? The case is already closed." He then asked himself what answer he should make. After a brief pause he decided that his best course would be to speak frankly, just as he had always done.

"As the district attorney knows," he began, smiling innocently, "I went into the room on only one occasion. That was two days before the murder. However, now that I come to think of it, I do remember that screen distinctly, and I can say that, when I saw it, it was *not* damaged."

"Are you absolutely sure of this?" Dr. Akechi quickly asked. "Remember now, the damage I mean is a scratch on the face of Komachi painted on the screen."

"Yes, yes, I know," Fukiya said emphatically. "And I'm positive, I tell you, that there was no scratch, neither on the face of the beautiful Komachi nor anywhere else. If it had been damaged in any way, I'm sure I could not have failed to notice it."

"Well, then, would you mind making an affidavit?" Dr. Akechi shot back. "You see, the owner of the screen is very insistent in his demand, and I find it very difficult to deal with him."

"Not at all," Fukiya said, in his most cooperative tone. "I would be most willing to make an affidavit any time you say."

Dr. Akechi thanked the student with a smile, then scratched his head, a habit of his whenever he was excited. "And now," he continued, "I think you can admit that you know a great deal about the screen, because in the record of your psychological test, I noticed that you replied 'screen' to 'picture.' A screen, as you know, is something rare in a student boardinghouse."

Fukiya was surprised at Dr. Akechi's new tone. He wondered what the devil the man was trying to get at.

Again the man who had been introduced as a lawyer addressed him. "By the way," he said, "there was still another point which came to my attention. When the psychological test was conducted yesterday, there were eight highly significant danger words on the list. You, of course, passed the test without a hitch. In fact, in my opinion, it went off altogether *too* smoothly. With your permission I'd like to have you take a look at your record on those eight key words."

Dr. Akechi produced the tabulation of the results and said: "You took little less time to answer the key words than the insignificant words. For example, in answer to 'dwarf tree,' you said 'pine' in only six-tenths of a second. This indicates remarkable innocence. Note that you took one-tenth of a second longer to answer to the word 'green,' which of all the twenty-eight words on the list is generally the easiest to respond to."

Not quite understanding Dr. Akechi's motive, Fukiya began to wonder where all this talk was leading. Just what was this talkative lawyer up to, anyway, he asked himself with a shudder. He had to know, and quickly, for it might be a trap.

"'Dwarf tree,' 'oilpaper,' 'crime,' or any other of the eight key words are not nearly so easy to associate with other words as are such words as 'head' or 'green,'" Dr. Akechi continued tenaciously. "And yet, you managed to answer the difficult words quicker than the easier ones. What does it all mean? This is what puzzled me all along. But now, let me try to guess exactly what was in your mind. Really, you know, it might prove to be quite amusing. Of course, if I'm wrong, I humbly beg your pardon."

Fukiya felt a cold shiver run down his spine. This weird business was now really beginning to prey on his nerves. But before he could even attempt to interrupt, Dr. Akechi began speaking again.

"Surely you have been well aware all along of the dangers of a psychological test," he insisted to Fukiya. "I take it, therefore, that you prepared yourself for the test well in advance. For example, for all words associated with the crime, you carefully drafted ready-made replies, so that you could recite them at a moment's notice. Now, please don't misunderstand, Mr. Fukiya. I am not trying to criticize the method you adopted. I only want to point out that a psychological test is a dangerous experiment on occasions. More often than not, it snares the innocent, and frees the guilty."

Dr. Akechi paused to let the hidden implications of his statements sink in, then he resumed again.

"You, Mr. Fukiya, made the fatal mistake of making your preparations with too much cunning. When you were confronted with the test, you spoke too fast. This, of course, was only natural, because you were afraid that if you took too much time in answering the questions, you would be suspected. But . . . you overdid it!"

Dr. Akechi paused again, noting with grim satisfaction that Fukiya's face was turning a sickly gray. Then he continued his summation:

"I come now to another significant phase of the test. Why did you choose to reply with such words as 'money,' 'conceal,' and 'murder'—all words which were liable to incriminate you? I will tell you. It was because you purposely wanted to make out that you were naive. Am I not right, Fukiya? Isn't my reasoning sound?"

Fukiya stared with glassy eyes at the face of his tormentor. He tried hard to look away, to evade the cold, accusing eyes of Dr. Akechi; but for some reason he found he couldn't. It appeared to Kasamori as though Fukiya had been caught in a hypnotic trance and was unable to manifest any emotion other than fear.

"This seeming innocence of yours," Dr. Akechi continued, "just did not strike me as being truly genuine. So I thought up the idea of asking you about the gold screen. Of course, the answer you gave was exactly the one I anticipated."

Dr. Akechi suddenly turned to the district attorney. "Now, I want to ask you a simple question, Mr. District Attorney. Just *when* was the screen brought into the house of the old woman?"

"The day before the crime, on the fourth of last month," Kasamori replied.

"The day before the crime, did you say?" Dr. Akechi repeated loudly. "But that's very strange. Mr. Fukiya just stated a moment ago that he saw it *two days before* the crime was committed, which was the third of last month. Furthermore, he was very positive as to where he had seen it—in the very room where the old woman was murdered! Now, this is all very contradictory. Surely, one of you two must be mistaken!"

"Mr. Fukiya must be the one who has made the miscalculation," observed the district attorney with a sly grin. "Until the afternoon of the fourth the screen was at the house of the owner. There is no question about it!"

Dr. Akechi watched Fukiya's face with rapt interest, for the expression that the latter now wore was akin to that of a little girl on the verge of tears.

Suddenly Dr. Akechi pointed an accusing finger at the student, and demanded sharply "Why did you say you saw something which you could not have seen? It's really too bad that you had to remember the classical painting, because by doing so you have betrayed yourself! In your anxiety to pretend to tell the truth, you even tried to elaborate on the details. Isn't this so, Fukiya? Could you have noticed that there was no folding screen in the room when you entered it two days before the crime? No, you certainly would not have paid any attention to such a detail, because it had nothing to do with your plans. Furthermore, I think that even if it had been there, it would not have attracted your attention, because the room was elaborately decorated with various other paintings and antiques of a similar nature. So it was quite natural for you to assume that the screen which you saw on the day of the crime must have been there two days previously. My questions bewildered you, so you accepted their implications. Now, had you been an ordinary criminal, you would not have answered as you did. You would have tried to deny knowing anything about anything. But I had you sized up from the very beginning as being a real intellectual, and as such, I knew you would try to be as outspoken as possible so long as you did not touch upon anything dangerous. But I anticipated your moves, and played my hand accordingly."

Dr. Akechi then broke out into loud, boisterous laughter. "Too bad," he said sarcastically to the crestfallen Fukiya, "that you had to be trapped by a humble lawyer like myself."

Fukiya remained silent, knowing that it would be useless to try and talk his way out. Clever as he was, he realized that any attempt to correct the fatal slip he had made would only drag him deeper and deeper into the pit of doom.

After a long silence, Dr. Akechi spoke again. "Can you hear the scratching of pen against paper, Fukiya? A police stenographer in the next room has been recording everything we've said here."

He called out to someone in the adjoining room, and a moment later a young stenographer entered the study, carrying a sheaf of papers.

"Please read your notes," Dr. Akechi requested.

The stenographer read the complete record, taken down word for word.

"Now, Mr. Fukiya," Dr. Akechi said, "I would appreciate it if you will kindly sign the document, and seal it with your fingerprint. Certainly you can have no objection, for you promised to testify regarding the screen at any time."

Meekly, Fukiya signed the record and sealed it with an imprint of his thumb. A few moments later, several detectives from police headquarters, summoned by the district attorney, led the confessed slayer away.

The show now over, Dr. Akechi turned to the district attorney. "As I have remarked before," he said, "Muensterberg was right when he said that the true merit of a psychological test lies in the discovery of whether or not a suspected person noticed any other person, or thing, at a certain place. In Fukiya's case, everything hinged on whether or not he had seen the screen. Apart from establishing that fact, no psychological test that you might have given Fukiya would have brought any remarkable results. Being the intellectual scoundrel he is, his mind was too well prepared to be defeated by any routine psychological questions."

Rising from his seat with the air of a professor leaving his class following a lengthy lecture, Dr. Akechi put on his hat, then paused briefly for a final statement.

"Just one more thing I would like to mention," he said with a smile. "In conducting a psychological test, there is no need for strange charts, machines, or word games. As discovered by the famous Judge Ooka, in the colorful days of eighteenth-century Tokyo, who frequently applied psychological tests based on mere questions and answers, it's not too difficult to catch criminals in psychological traps. But of course, you have to ask the right questions. Well good night, Mr. District Attorney. And thanks for the refreshments."

The Caterpillar

Tokiko said goodbye, left the main house, and went into the twilight through the wide, utterly neglected garden overgrown with weeds, toward the detached cottage where she and her husband lived. While walking, she recalled the conventional words of praise which had been again bestowed upon her a few moments ago by the retired major general who was the master of the main house.

Somehow she felt very queer, and a bitter taste much akin to that of broiled eggplant, which she positively detested, remained in her mouth.

"The loyalty and meritorious services of Lieutenant Sunaga are of course the boast of our Army," he had stated. (The old general was ludicrous enough to continue to dignify her disabled soldier husband with his old title.)

"As for you, however, your continued faithfulness has deprived you of all your former pleasures and desires. For three long years you have sacrificed everything for that poor crippled man, without emitting the faintest breath of complaint. You always contend that this is but the natural duty of a soldier's wife, and so it is. But I sometimes cannot help feeling that it's a cruel fate for a woman to endure, especially for a woman so

[Certain archaic terms have been amended. Ed.]

very attractive and charming as you, and so young, too. I am quite struck with admiration. I honestly believe it to be one of the most stirring human-interest stories of the day. The question which still remains is: How long will it last? Remember, you still have quite a long future ahead of you. For your husband's sake, I pray that you will never change."

Old Major General Washio always liked to sing the praises of the disabled Lieutenant Sunaga (who had once been on his staff and was now his guest tenant) and his wife, so much so that it had become a well-rehearsed line of conversation whenever he saw her. But this was all extremely distasteful to Tokiko, and she tried to avoid the general as much as possible. Occasionally, when the tedium of life with her silent, crippled husband became unbearable, she would seek the company of the general's wife and daughter, but usually only after first making sure that the general was absent.

Secretly, she felt that her self-sacrificing spirit and rare faithfulness well deserved the old man's lavish praise, and at first this had tickled her vanity. But in those early days the whole arrangement had been a novelty. Then it had even been fun, in a way, to care for one so completely helpless as her husband.

Gradually, however, her self-satisfaction had begun to change into boredom, and then into fear. Now she shuddered whenever she was highly praised. She imagined she could see an accusing finger pointing at her, while in her ear she heard a sarcastic voice rasping: "Under the cloak of faithfulness you are leading a life of sin and treachery!"

Day by day the unconscious changes which took place in her way of thinking surprised even herself. In fact, she often wondered at the fickleness of human feelings.

In the beginning she had been only a humble and faithful wife, ignorant of the world, naive and bashful in the extreme. But now, although her outward appearance showed little change, horrible passions dwelt in her heart, passions awak-

ened by the constant sight of her pitiful, crippled husband—
he was so crippled that the word was utterly inappropriate to
describe his condition—he who had once been so proud, and
of such a noble bearing.

Like a beast of prey, or as if possessed by the devil, she had
begun to feel an insane urge to gratify her lust! Yes, she had
changed—so completely! From where did this maddening impulse spring, she asked herself. Could it be attributed to the
mysterious charm of that lump of flesh? As a matter of fact,
that is all her husband was—just a lump of flesh! Or was it the
work of some uncanny, supernatural power which could not
be defined?

Whenever General Washio spoke to her, Tokiko could not
help feeling conscious of this inexplicable sense of guilt. Furthermore, she became more and more conscious of her own
large and fat body.

"An alarming situation," she kept repeating. "Why do I continue to grow so fat like some lazy fool?" In sharp contrast,
however, her countenance was very pale, and she often seemed
to sense that the general looked upon her body dubiously
while uttering his usual words of praise. Perhaps this was why
she detested him.

It was a remote district where they lived, and the distance
from the main house to the cottage was almost half a city block.
Between the houses there was a grassy field with no regular
paths, where striped snakes often crawled out with rustling
noises. Also, if one took a false step, he was immediately in danger of falling into an old abandoned well covered with weeds.
An uneven apology for a hedge surrounded the large mansion,
with fields sprawling beyond it.

From the darkness where she stood Tokiko eyed the gaunt,
two-storied cottage, their abode, with its back towards the far
grove of a small Buddhist shrine. In the sky a couple of stars
seemed to twinkle a little more brightly than the others. The

room where her husband lay was dark. He was naturally unable to light the lamp, and so the "lump of flesh" must be blinking his eyes helplessly, leaning back in his squat chair, or slipping off the seat to lie on the mats in the gloom.

What a pity! When she thought of it, chills of disgust, misery, and sorrow seemed to run down her spine.

Entering the house, she noticed that the door of the room upstairs was ajar, gaping like a wide black mouth, and she heard the familiar low sound of tapping on the mats.

"Oh, he is at it again," she said to herself, and she suddenly felt so sorry for him that tears sprang to her eyes. These sounds meant that her disabled husband was lying on his back, calling impatiently for his only companion by beating his head against the matted floor instead of clapping hands like any ordinary Japanese husband would.

"I'm coming now. You must be hungry." She spoke softly in her usual manner, even though she knew that she could not be heard. Then she climbed the ladder-like stairs to the small room on the second floor.

In the room there was an alcove, with an old-fashioned lamp in one corner. Beside it there was a box of matches, but he was unable to strike a light.

In the tone of a mother speaking to her baby, she said: "I've kept you waiting a long time, haven't I? I'm so sorry." Then she added: "Be patient now for just a moment. I can do nothing in this darkness. I'm going to light the lamp."

Although she kept muttering thus, she knew her husband could hear nothing. After lighting the lamp, she brought it to the desk in another corner of the room. In front of the desk was a low chair, to which was fastened a printed-muslin cushion. The chair was vacant, and its erstwhile occupant was now on the matted floor—a strange, gruesome creature. It was dressed—"was wrapped" might be more appropriate—in old silken robes.

Yes, there "it" was, a large, living parcel wrapped in silken kimono, looking like a parcel which someone had discarded, an odd bundle indeed!

From one part of the parcel protruded the head of a man, which kept tapping against the mat like a spring-beetle or some strange automatic machine. As it tapped, the large bundle moved bit by bit . . . like a crawling worm.

"You mustn't lose your temper like that. What do you want? This?" She made the gesture of taking food. "No? Then this?"

She tried another gesture, but her mute husband shook his head every time and continued to knock his head desperately against the matting.

His whole face had been so badly shattered by the splinters of a shell that it was just like a mass of putty. Only upon close observation could one recognize it as once having been a human face.

The left ear was entirely gone, and only a small black hole showed where it had once been. From the left side of his mouth across his cheek to beneath his eyes there was a pronounced twitch like a suture, while an ugly scar also crept across his right temple up to the top of his head. His throat caved in as if the flesh there had been scooped out, while his nose and mouth retained nothing of their original shapes.

In this monstrous face, however, there were still set two bright, round eyes like those of an innocent child, contrasting sharply with the ugliness around them. Just now they were gleaming with irritation.

"Ah! You want to say something to me, don't you? Wait a minute."

She took a notebook and pencil out of the drawer of the desk, put the pencil in his deformed mouth and held the opened notebook against it. Her husband could neither speak nor hold a pen, for as he had no vocal organs, he likewise had no arms or legs.

"Tired of me?" These were the words the cripple scrawled with his mouth.

"Ho, ho, ho! You're jealous again, aren't you?" she laughed. "Don't be a little fool."

But the cripple again began to strike his head impatiently against the mat floor. Tokiko understood what he meant and again pressed the notebook against the point of the pencil held between his teeth.

Once more the pencil moved unsteadily and wrote: "Where go?"

As soon as she looked at it, Tokiko roughly snatched the pencil away from the man's mouth, wrote: "To the Washios'," and almost pushed the written reply against his eyes.

As he read the curt note, she added: "You should know! What other place have I to go?"

The cripple again called for the notebook and wrote: "3 hours?"

A surge of sympathy again swept over her. "I didn't realize I was away so long," she wrote back. "I'm sorry."

She expressed her pity, bowed, and waved her hand, saying: "I won't go again. I won't ever go again. I promise."

Lieutenant Sunaga, or rather "the bundle," still seemed far from satisfied, but perhaps he became tired of the performance of writing with his mouth, for his head lay limp on the floor and moved no more. After a brief spell, he looked hard at her, putting every meaning into his large eyes.

Tokiko knew just one way to soothe her husband's temper. As words and excuses were of no avail, whenever they had their strange "lovers' quarrels," she resorted to this more expedient act.

Suddenly bending over her husband, she smothered his twisted mouth with kisses. Soon, a look of deep contentment and pleasure crept into his eyes, followed by an ugly smile. She continued to kiss him—closing her eyes in order to forget his ugliness—and, gradually, she felt a strong urge to tease this poor cripple, who was so utterly helpless.

The cripple, kissed with such passion, writhed in the agony of being unable to breathe and distorted his face oddly. As always, this sight excited Tokiko strangely.

In the medical world the case of Lieutenant Sunaga had created quite a stir. His arms and legs had been amputated and his face skilfully patched up by the surgeons. As for the newspapers, they had also played up the story, and one journal had even spoken of him as "the pathetic broken doll whose precious limbs were cruelly torn off by the playful gods of war."

Lieutenant Sunaga was all the more pitiful in that, although he was a fourfold amputee, his torso was extremely well developed. Possibly because of his keen appetite—eating was his only diversion—Sunaga's belly was glossy and bulging. In fact, the man was just like a large yellow caterpillar.

His arms and legs had been amputated so closely that not even stumps remained, but only four lumps of flesh to mark where his limbs had been. Often he would lie on his great belly and, using these lumps to propel himself, manage to spin round and round—a top made of living flesh.

After a time Tokiko began to strip him naked. He offered no resistance, but just lay looking expectantly into those strangely narrowed eyes of hers, like the eyes with which an animal watches its prey.

Tokiko well understood what her crippled husband wanted to say with his amorous eyes. Lieutenant Sunaga had lost every sensory organ except those of sight, feeling, and taste. He had never had much liking for books, and furthermore, his wits had been dulled by the shock of the explosion to which he had fallen victim. So now even the pastime of reading had been given up, and physical pleasures were his only diversion.

As for Tokiko, although hers was a timid heart, she had always entertained a strange liking for bullying the weak.

Moreover, watching the agony of this poor cripple aroused many of her hidden impulses.

Still leaning over him, she continued her aberrant caresses, stirring the crippled man's feeling to ever higher frenzies of passion. . . .

Tokiko shrieked and woke up. She had had a terrible nightmare, and now she found herself sitting up in a cold sweat. The lamp at her bedside was blackened with smoke, the wick burned down to its base.

The interior of the room, the ceilings, the walls. . . all seemed to be stretching like rubber, and then contracting into strange shapes. The face of her husband beside her was of a glossy orange hue.

She reminded herself that he positively could not have heard her shriek, but she noticed with uneasiness that he was gazing at the ceiling, his bright eyes wide open. She looked at the clock on the desk and noted that it was a little past one.

Now that she was wide awake she tried to erase all thoughts of the horrors of the nightmare that had assailed her mind, but the more she tried to forget, the more persistent became the images. First a mist seemed to rise before her eyes, and when this cleared, she could distinctly see a large lump of flesh, floating in mid-air, spinning and spinning like a top. Suddenly a stout, ugly woman's body seemed to appear from nowhere, and the two figures became interlocked in a mad embrace. The weirdly erotic scene reminded Tokiko of a picture postcard portraying a section of Dante's Inferno; and yet, as her mind drifted, the very disgust and ugliness of the embracing pair seemed to excite all her pent-up passions and to paralyze her nerves. With a shudder she asked herself if she were sexually perverted.

Holding her breasts, she suddenly uttered a piercing cry. Then she looked at her husband intently, like a child gazing at a broken doll. He was still looking at the same spot on the ceiling, taking absolutely no notice of her.

"He is thinking again," she told herself.

Even at the best of times it was an eerie thing to see a man whose only organ of communication was his eyes lie there with those eyes fixed forever on just one spot, and now how much more so in the middle of the night. Of course his mind has become dull, she thought, but for a man so completely crippled as he, there undoubtedly exists a world completely different from any I can ever know. Is it a pleasant world, she wondered. Or is it a hell. . . .

For a while she closed her eyes again and tried to sleep, but she found it impossible. She felt as if flames were whirling around her with roaring sounds, and her mind ached. Time and again various illusions and hallucinations would wantonly appear and then vanish. Into them were woven the manifold tragic happenings which had changed her normal life into this miserable existence since three years back. . . .

When she first received the news that her husband had been wounded and would be sent back to Japan, she felt indescribably relieved to know that at least his life had been spared. The wives of his fellow officers even envied her "good fortune."

Presently the distinguished services rendered by her husband were written up in the newspapers. She knew at the time that his wounds were serious, but she never imagined for a moment that he had been crippled to such an extent.

Never would she forget the first time she was permitted to visit her husband in the garrison hospital. His face was completely covered with bandages, and there was nothing but his eyes, gazing at her vacantly. She remembered how bitterly she wept when they told her that his wounds and the shock had left him both deaf and dumb. Little did she dream, however, of the horrible discoveries that were still to come.

The head physician, dignified as he was, tried to appear deeply sympathetic and turned up the white bed-sheets cautiously. "Try to be brave!" were his very words.

She tried to clasp her husband's hands—but could find no arms. Then she discovered that his legs were also missing; he was like a ghost in a bad dream. Beneath the sheets there lay only his trunk, bandaged grotesquely, like a mummy.

She tried to speak, and then to scream, but no sounds came out of her throat. She, too, had been rendered momentarily speechless. God! Was this all that was left of the husband she loved so dearly! He was no longer a man, but only a plaster bust.

It was after she had been shown to another room by the head physician and nurses that she completely broke down, bursting into loud weeping despite the presence of the others. Throwing herself down on a chair, she buried her head in her arms and wept till her tears ran utterly dry.

"It was a real miracle," she heard the physician say. "No other person could possibly have survived. Of course it's all the result of Colonel Kitamura's wonderful surgical skill—he's a real genius with the operating knife. There's probably no other such example in any garrison hospital in any country."

Thus the physician tried to console Tokiko. The word "miracle" was continually repeated, but she did not know whether to rejoice or grieve.

About half a year had passed in a dream. The "living corpse" of Lieutenant Sunaga was eventually escorted home by his commanding officer and comrades in arms, and everyone made quite a fuss over him.

In the days that followed, Tokiko nursed him with tender care, shedding endless tears. Relatives, neighbors, and friends all urged her on to greater self-sacrifice, constantly dinning their definitions of "honor" and "virtue" into her ears. Her husband's meager pension was scarcely enough to keep them, so when Major General Washio, Sunaga's former commanding officer at the front, kindly offered to let them live in the detached cottage on his country estate free of charge, they accepted gratefully.

From then on their daily life became routine, but this too brought maddening loneliness. The quiet environment, of course, was a prime cause. Another was the fact that people were no longer interested in the story of the crippled war hero and his dutiful wife. It was stale news; new personalities and events were commanding their interest.

Her husband's relatives seldom came to call. On her side, both her parents were dead, while all her sisters and brothers were indifferent to her sorrows. As a result the poor crippled soldier and his faithful wife lived alone in the solitary cottage in the country, completely isolated from the outside world. But even this state of affairs would not have been so bad if one of them had not been like a doll made of clay.

Lieutenant Sunaga was at first quite confused. Although aware of his tragic plight, his gradual return to normal health brought with it feelings of remorse, melancholy, and complete despair.

Whatever Tokiko and her husband said to each other was through the medium of the written word. The first words he wrote were "newspaper" and "decoration." By the first he meant that he wanted to see the clippings of the papers which had carried the story of his glorious record; and by "decoration" he was asking to see the Order of the Golden Kite, Japan's highest military decoration, which he had been awarded. These had been the first things Major General Washio had thrust before his eyes when he had recovered consciousness at the hospital, and he remembered them.

After that the crippled man often wrote the same words and asked for the two items, and each time Tokiko held them before him, he gazed long at them. Tokiko felt rather silly while he read the newspapers over and over, but she did derive some pleasure from the look of deep satisfaction in her husband's eyes. Often she held the clippings and the decoration until her hands became quite numb.

As time passed, Lieutenant Sunaga became bored with the term "honor." After a while he no longer asked for the relics of his war record. Instead, his requests turned more and more frequently toward food, for despite his deformity, his appetite grew ever larger. In fact, he was as greedy for food as a patient recovering from some alimentary disorder. If Tokiko did not immediately comply with his request, he would give vent to his temper by crawling about madly on the mats.

At first Tokiko felt a vague fear of his uncouth manners and disliked them, but in time she grew used to his strange whims. With the two completely shut up in the solitary cottage in the country, if one of them had not compromised, life would have become unbearable. So, like two animals caged in a zoo, they pursued their lonely existence.

Thus, from every viewpoint, it was only natural that Tokiko should come to look upon her husband as a big toy, to be played with as she pleased. Furthermore, her crippled husband's greed had infected her own character to the point where she too had become extremely avaricious.

There seemed to be but one consolation for her miserable "career" as nursemaid to a cripple: the very fact that this poor, strange thing which not only could neither speak nor hear, but could not even move freely by itself, was by no means made of wood or clay, but was alive and real, possessing every human emotion and instinct—this was a source of boundless fascination for her. Still further, those round eyes of his, which comprised his only expressive organ, speaking so sadly sometimes, and sometimes so angrily—these too had a strange charm. The pitiful thing was that he was incapable of wiping away the tears which those eyes could still shed. And of course, when he was angry, he had no power to threaten her other than that of working himself into an abnormal heat of frenzy. These fits of wrath usually came on whenever he was reminded that he would never again be able to succumb, of his own free will, to the one overwhelming temptation which was always lurking within him.

Meanwhile, Tokiko also managed to find a secondary source of pleasure in tormenting this helpless creature whenever she felt like it. Cruel? Yes! But it was fun—great fun! . . .

These happenings of the past three years were vividly reflected inside Tokiko's closed eyelids, as though cast by a magic lantern, the fragmentary memories forming themselves in her mind and fading away one after the other. This was a phenomenon which occurred whenever there was something wrong with her body. On such occasions, especially during her monthly periods of physical indisposition, she would maltreat the poor cripple with real venom. The barbarity of her actions had grown wilder and more intense with the progress of time. She was, of course, fully aware of the criminal nature of her deeds, but the wild forces rising inside her body were beyond the control of her will.

Suddenly she felt that the interior of the room was becoming darker, that another nightmare was about to overtake her. But this time she determined to see it with her eyes open. The thought frightened her, and her heart began to skip beats. But she calmed her mind and persuaded herself that she was prone to imagine things. The wick of the lamp at her bedside was spent, and the light was flickering. Climbing out of bed, she turned the wick high.

Quickly the room brightened up, but the light of the lamp was blurred in colors of orange, and this increased her uneasiness. By the same light Tokiko looked again at her husband's face, and was startled to see that his eyes were still fixed on the same spot on the ceiling, not having changed position even a fraction of an inch!

"What could he possibly be thinking about?" she asked herself with a shiver. Although she felt extremely uneasy, hers was even more a feeling of intense hatred of his attitude. Her hatred again awakened all her inherent desires to torment him—to make him suffer.

Suddenly, without any warning, she threw herself upon her husband's bed, grabbed his shoulders with her large hands, and began to shake him furiously.

Startled by this sudden violence, the crippled man began to tremble. Biting his lip, he stared at her fiercely.

"Are you angry? Why do you look at me like that?" Tokiko asked sarcastically. "It's no use getting angry, you know! You're quite at my mercy."

Sunaga could not reply, but the words that might have come to his lips showed from his penetrating eyes.

"Your eyes are mad!" Tokiko shrieked. "Don't stare at me like that!"

On a sudden impulse she thrust her fingers roughly into his eyes, shouting: "Now try to stare if you can!"

The cripple struggled desperately, his torso writhing and twisting, and his intense suffering finally gave him the strength to lift his trunk and send her sprawling backward.

Quickly Tokiko regained her balance and turned to resume her attack. But suddenly she stopped. . . . Horror of horrors! From both her husband's eyes blood was spurting; his face, twitching in pain, had the pallor of a boiled octopus.

Tokiko was paralyzed with fear. She had cruelly deprived her husband of his only window to the outside world. What was left to him now? Nothing, absolutely nothing . . . just his mass of ghastly flesh, in total darkness.

Stumbling downstairs, she staggered out into the dark night barefooted. Passing through the back gate of the garden, she rushed out onto the village road, running as though in a nightmare pursued by specters—fast and yet seeming not to move.

Eventually she reached her destination—the lone house of a country doctor. After hearing her hysterical story, the doctor accompanied her back to the cottage.

In the room her husband was still struggling violently, suffering the tortures of hell. The doctor had often heard of the limbless man, but had never seen him before; he was shocked beyond words by the gruesome sight of the cripple. After giving him an injection to relieve his pain, he dressed the blinded eyes and then hurried away, not even asking for any explanation of the "accident."

By the time Lieutenant Sunaga stopped struggling it was already dawn. Caressing his chest tenderly, Tokiko shed big drops of tears and implored: "Forgive me, my darling. Please forgive me."

The lump of flesh was stricken with fever, its red face swollen and its heart beating rapidly.

Tokiko did not leave the bedside of her patient all day, not even to take any food. She kept squeezing out wet cloths for his head; and in the brief intervals she wrote "Forgive me" again and again on her husband's chest with her finger. She was utterly unconscious of the passing of time.

By evening the patient's temperature showed a slight drop, and his breathing seemed to return to normal. Tokiko surmised he must also have regained consciousness, so again she wrote "Forgive me" on his chest. The lump of flesh, however, made no attempt to make any kind of a reply. Although he had lost his eyes, it would still have been possible for him to answer her signals in some way, either by shaking his head or by smiling. But his facial expression remained unchanged. By the sound of his breathing she knew for sure he was not asleep, but it was impossible to tell whether he had also lost the ability to understand the message traced on his chest or was only keeping silent out of anger.

While gazing at him, Tokiko could not help trembling with terror. This "thing" that lay before her was indeed a living creature. He had lungs and a stomach as well as a heart. Nevertheless, he could not see anything; he could not hear anything; he could not speak a word; he had no limbs. His world was a bottomless pit of perpetual silence and boundless darkness. Who could imagine such a terrible world? With what could the feelings of a man living in that abyss be compared? Surely he must crave to shout for help at the top of his lungs . . . to see shapes, no matter how dim . . . to hear voices, even the faintest of whispers . . . to cling to something . . . to grasp. . . .

Suddenly Tokiko burst out crying with remorse over the irreparable crime she had committed. Fear and sorrow gnawing at her heart, she left her husband there and ran to the Washios in the main house: she wanted to see a human face—any face that was not deformed.

The old general listened anxiously to her long confession, made incoherent at times by fits of weeping, and when she was through he was momentarily too astounded to utter a word. After a while he said he would visit the lieutenant immediately.

As it was already dark, a lantern was prepared for the old man. He and Tokiko plodded through the grassy field toward the cottage, both silent and engrossed in their own thoughts.

When they finally reached the ill-omened room the old man looked inside and then exclaimed: "Nobody's here! Where's he gone?"

Tokiko, however, was not alarmed. "He must be in his bed," she said.

She went to the bed in the semi-gloom, but found it empty.

"No!" she cried. "He—he isn't here!"

"He couldn't have gone out," reasoned the general. "We must search the house."

After a thorough search of every nook and corner had proved quite fruitless, General Washio had to admit that his former subordinate was indeed not in the house.

Suddenly Tokiko discovered a penciled scrawl on one of the paper doors.

"Look!" she said with a puzzled frown, pointing to the scrawl. "What's this?"

They both stooped to look. After a few moments spent deciphering the almost illegible scribble, she made out the message.

"I forgive you!" it said.

Tears immediately welled in Tokiko's eyes, and she began to feel dizzy. It was evident that her husband had managed to drag his truncated body across the room, picked up a pencil from the low desk in his mouth, laboriously written the curt message, and then—

Suddenly Tokiko came alive with action.

"Quick!" she shouted, her face paling. "He may be committing suicide!"

The Washio household was quickly aroused, and soon servants came out with lanterns to search the field. Hither and thither they looked, trampling down the weeds between the main house and the cottage.

Tokiko anxiously followed old man Washio in the dim light of the lantern which he held. While she walked the words "I forgive you" kept leaping to her mind; clearly this was his answer to the message she had traced on his chest. Turning the words over and over in her mind, she came to realize that his message also meant: "I'm going to die. But do not grieve, because I have forgiven you!"

What a heartless witch she had been! In her mind's eye she could vividly see her limbless husband falling down the stairs and crawling out into the darkness. She felt that she would choke with sorrow and remorse.

After they had walked about for some time, a horrible thought struck her. Turning to the general, she ventured; "There is an old well hereabouts, isn't there?"

"Yes," he replied gravely, immediately understanding what she meant.

Both of them hurried in a new direction.

"The well should be around here, I think," said the old man finally, as if talking to himself. Then he held up his lantern to spread as much light as possible.

Just then Tokiko was struck by some uncanny intuition. She stopped in her tracks. Straining her ears, she heard a faint rustling sound like that made by a snake crawling through the grass.

She and the old man looked toward the sound, and almost simultaneously they both became transfixed with fear.

In the dim light a black thing was wriggling sluggishly in the thick growth of weeds. Suddenly the thing raised its head and crawled forward, scraping the ground with projections like excrescences at the four corners of its body. It advanced stealthily inch by inch.

After a time the upraised head suddenly disappeared into the ground, dragging its whole body after it. A few seconds later they heard the faint sound of a splash far beneath the ground in what seemed like the bowels of the earth.

Tokiko and the general finally mustered enough courage to step forward. . . and there, hidden in the grass, they found the old well, its black mouth gaping.

Strangely enough, in those timeless moments it had been the image of a caterpillar which had flashed again into Tokiko's mind—a bloated creature slowly creeping along the dead branch of a gaunt tree on a dark night . . . inching its way to the end of the branch and then suddenly dropping off . . . falling down . . . down into the boundless darkness beneath.

The Cliff

he season is spring. Atop a cliff, about a mile from K——Spa,
two persons are sitting on a rock. Far below them in the valley
can faintly be heard the babbling water of a river. The man
is in his mid-twenties, the woman slightly older. Both are wearing the
padded outer kimono of a hot-spring hotel.

Woman: Isn't it odd that in all this time we've never discussed
those incidents that keep preying on our minds so.
Sometimes I think I'll suffocate if I don't discuss
them. Since we have so much free time today, let's
talk about those things of the past a little. You won't
mind, will you, darling?

Man: Of course not, my dear. You go ahead, and I'll add my
comments from time to time.

Woman: Well, let's see. . . . To begin at the beginning, there
was that night when I was lying in bed, side by side
with Saito. He was weeping as usual, with his face
pressed against mine, and his tears kept trickling into
my mouth—

[Certain archaic terms have been amended. Ed.]

Man: Don't be so explicit! I don't want to hear the details of your intimacies with your first husband.

Woman: But this is an important part of the story, because that was when I first had a clear insight into his plans. But all right—for your sake I'll omit the details. . . . So, it was just as I tasted the salt of his tears that I suddenly told myself something was amiss. The way he was crying that night was far more intense than usual, as if he had some hidden reason. Startled, I drew back and looked into his tear-stained eyes.

Man: That must have made your blood run cold—to have your married happiness suddenly turn into fear. I remember your telling me that he seemed to have pity in his eyes as he returned your look.

Woman: Yes, his eyes spoke eloquently of the pity he felt for me. I believe a man's innermost secrets can be read in his eyes. And on this occasion certainly, Saito's eyes were so eloquent that I perceived his thoughts instantly.

Man: He was planning to kill you, wasn't he?

Woman: Yes. But, of course, the whole thing was only a sort of game for him. In many ways he was a sadist, as you know, and I was just the opposite. I'm sure that's why he wanted to play the game. There's no denying that we loved each other, but we both incessantly craved for more excitement.

Man: I know, I know! You needn't say any more.

Woman: That night was the first time I felt I could plainly read his mind. Vague suspicions had disturbed me for some time, but now real fear gripped my heart. I shuddered to think he would go to such lengths. But I was thrilled in spite of my fears.

Man: That look of pity you saw in his eyes—that was part of the game too, wasn't it? He wanted you to be frightened, and this was his way of hinting at what was in store for you. And then—

Woman: Then there was the man in the blue overcoat.

Man: Yes, with a blue felt hat, dark glasses, and a thick mustache.

Woman: You had seen him before, hadn't you?

Man: Yes, there I was, a striving painter boarding at your house, playing the role of a clown in the midst of your and your husband's affairs. It was one day while I was out roaming the streets that the man first attracted my attention. And when I asked the owner of the teahouse on the corner, she told me the stranger had been asking a lot of questions about your house.

Woman: It was after you brought me this news that I happened to see him myself. The first time was outside my kitchen, and twice more near the front gate. Each time he was standing like a shadow, dressed in his baggy overcoat, both his hands shoved deep in his pockets.

Man: I thought he was a sneak thief at first, and several servants in the neighborhood also warned me about him.

Woman: But he turned out to be much worse, a far more dangerous character than a mere sneak thief, didn't he? Somehow, that dreadful night, his sinister form leapt to my mind the instant I gazed into my husband's tear-stained eyes.

Man: And then you had a third hint of his plans, didn't you?

Woman: Yes, those detective stories you started bringing us. We'd read detective stories before, of course, but you really aroused our interest in the art of crime. It all started a few months before we saw the mysterious stranger, and almost every night we used to discuss nothing but various successful crimes. Saito, my husband, of course, was the most enthusiastic of all, as you may recall.

Man: Yes, that was about the time he thought up the best plot of them all.

Woman: You mean that trick of dual personality. There certainly were a lot of different ways of creating a dual personality, weren't there? I remember that long list you made up.

Man: Thirty-three different ways, if I remember correctly.

Woman: But Saito was most impressed with the possibility of creating an utterly nonexistent character.

Man: The theory was a simple one. For example, if a man decided to commit a murder, he would first create an imaginary character far in advance of the crime. This character would be his double. His description would be simple, with, say, a false mustache, dark glasses, and conspicuous clothing. Then he would have this double of his establish a residence far removed from his real domicile, and he would proceed to live two lives. While the real character would supposedly be away at work, the double would be at *his* home, and vice versa. Matters would be even more simple in the event one of the two characters went away on a long trip. With the stage thus set, the murder could be committed at an opportune time, but immediately before the crime the imaginary character would make himself very obvious to several witnesses. And then, following the crime, he would vanish completely from the face of the earth. Beforehand, of course, he would have destroyed all incriminating evidence, such as his disguise. As a result, he would be permanently missing from his home, while the real character would merely resume his former way of life. Naturally, as the crime was committed by a nonexistent character it would be a perfect crime.

Woman: Saito kept talking about this until I thought he was going crazy. All this I recalled as I stared into his eyes. But there was one more clue to his hidden thoughts. It was that diary, which he had "hidden" for the express purpose of having me find it. But the diary was planted for me to read, so of course it didn't mention his real secrets. For example, there was not a word about his mistress.

Man: It was like crossing out lines in a letter to make sure they'd be read.

Woman: I read the diary from cover to cover. Several pages were devoted to the dual-personality idea. I was quite struck by his ingenious ideas. And I must say he was a wizard with the pen.

Man: Go on.

Woman: Well, those were the three clues I had. First, the look in his eyes; next, the man in the blue overcoat; and finally, the diary describing the dual-personality trick. But somehow I had the feeling that the picture was incomplete. There seemed to be no motive. You supplied this when you told me about his mistress. After that I could never look into his eyes without seeing there the reflection of some beautiful girl I imagined his mistress to be. At times I even thought I could smell her perfume on him.

Man: In other words, these four clues convinced you that he was planning to kill you so he could get the fortune you inherited from your father, and then live with his mistress.

Woman: Yes, but at the same time I knew he was only playing a game to frighten me.

Man: Yes, maybe that's what you thought, but his motive was real enough. His plan was to steal into your bedroom in disguise, kill you, and vanish. Later the real Saito would return, "discover" your murder, and play the delicate role of the grief-stricken husband.

Woman: Yes, but as I said before, it was only part of the same game to frighten me, and to enjoy the thrill of suspense. You can imagine what a horrible game it was! That was the thrill he was aiming for. It's surprising how all these details came to my mind with full clarity in the split second I stared into his eyes.

Man: But where was Saito supposed to draw the line? What was the actual purpose of his disguise as the man in the blue overcoat?

Woman: I think he really intended to steal into my bedroom in his disguise and frighten me out of my wits. Then, after enjoying my hysterics, he would burst out laughing.

Man: But that isn't the way it turned out, is it?

Woman: It certainly wasn't! Until then, everything had been more or less a joke. But what happened next nearly froze the blood in my veins. I shudder even to think about it.

Man: No more than I do. But go on—get it off your chest now that there's nobody to hear us.

Woman: All right. . . . Several more times he went into weeping hysterics in bed, and gradually I began to realize that I couldn't fathom the look in his eyes any longer. In fact, I no longer knew if he was playing a game, or . . .

Man: You—you began to suspect that he was really planning to kill you, didn't you?

Woman: Yes. Now his glassy, staring eyes seemed to be saying: "At first, I created an imaginary character to give you a wonderful thrill. But now, having played the game this far, I'm becoming confused. How simple it would be really to kill you, and yet remain utterly unsuspected. Besides, you have a large fortune . . . which would become mine. What a temptation! For really, you know, I love someone else far more than you. But I do pity you, really I do." In those tormenting nights my fears grew stronger and stronger. And it was about this time, with my thoughts in a turmoil as we grappled and tangled in the dark of the bedroom, that I began again to taste his salty tears trickling into my mouth.

Man: That's when you came to talk to me.

Woman: Yes, but you said I was hysterical and tried to laugh my fears away. But, in spite of your laughter, I saw a hidden shadow in your eyes, and I began to suspect that you had the same fears as I.

Man: You may have thought so, but that wasn't the case at all. You've always had the piercing eyes of a mind reader, haven't you? Not many people have your power of reading even the subconscious mind.

Woman: After that I was always afraid to look into his eyes. And even more I feared that he might be able to read *my* eyes. Gradually the thought of his pistol began to prey on my mind. . . . One evening I saw the man in the blue overcoat outside the gate again. It was almost dark, but I thought I could see him leering at me. A cold shiver ran down my spine. And that instant I again remembered the pistol—the one hidden in the drawer of Saito's desk.

Man: I also knew about that pistol. He knew it was against the law to keep firearms, but he kept it anyway, fully loaded, and hid it in one of his desk drawers—merely for the sake of having it, I thought.

Woman: It suddenly struck me that the man in the blue overcoat might have that pistol in his pocket. I went immediately to Saito's desk and examined the drawer. But the pistol was there, and I felt immensely relieved.

Then I had another thought. I said to myself: "Surely if the man is Saito in disguise, he wouldn't be such a fool as to use his own pistol. This means he must be planning to use a different weapon." And thus my fears kept growing all the more.

Man: So you decided to take that pistol for your own protection.

Woman: Yes, I took it out of the desk and kept it with me all the time. At night I even slept with it.

Man: The existence of that pistol was unfortunate. Because if it had not existed . . .

Woman: That's when I asked you what would happen to me if a man stole into my bedroom at night and I shot him, even if he hadn't been planning any crime. Remember?

Man: Yes, and if I remember correctly I told you this would constitute self-defense and would not be considered a crime. Later on I was sorry I'd told you this.

Woman: And then, sure enough, he finally came. It was past midnight. He climbed over the fence and stole into the house through the kitchen window. The first thing I knew, I saw my bedroom door opening slowly, and then I saw him. It was him, all right. He wore the same blue overcoat. His felt hat was pulled low, and his dark glasses covered his eyes—and that awful mustache! Now was the time! I pretended to be asleep, but stole a glance at him—and gripped the pistol. . . .

Man: And then?

Woman: I could almost hear my heart beating. I wanted—oh, how I wanted—to pull the trigger, but I waited. He was standing there in the doorway, both hands in his pockets. Somehow I felt that he knew I was only pretending to be asleep. For what seemed like an hour we both watched each other. I wanted to scream, to leap out of bed and flee, but I gritted my teeth and held myself in check.

Man: And then?

Woman: Suddenly he began to move toward my bed. I peeped out from under the bedclothes and saw his face looming beside the night lamp. He was cleverly disguised, but I could see that he was definitely Saito. His eyes behind the dark glasses seemed to be smiling. Gradually, his face came closer and closer. . . . I couldn't see the knife in his hand, but there was no mistaking that he meant to kill me. I turned the pistol slowly under the covers and aimed at his heart. Then I pulled the trigger. . . . That's what brought you and the maid running in, but by that time I had fainted.

Man: As soon as I saw the dead man, I knew what had happened. The knife was lying beside him.

Woman: So the police came, and a few days later you and I were summoned to the procurator's office. I told the whole story from beginning to end, with you as a witness, and they soon released me. It was the knife you'd found on the floor that proved I had killed Saito in self-defense. . . . After that I had a nervous breakdown and spent a month in bed. How I appreciated the way you came to see me every day, taking the place of the friends and relatives I didn't have. . . . You even took care of that matter of Saito's mistress for me. . . .

Man: And now, just imagine, a year has already passed. And we've already been married for over five months. . . . Well, let's get back to the inn.

Woman: No. There's more to talk about.

Man: Really? What else is there to say? Haven't we already covered the ground completely?

Woman: Yes, but so far we've only touched the surface of things.

Man: The surface of things? It seems to me that we've analyzed the matter quite thoroughly.

Woman: But you forget, my dear, that behind one curtain there's always another. . . .

Man: For the life of me I don't know what you mean. You're acting strangely today.

Woman: You're afraid, aren't you?

The man's face twitches, but his eyes remain expressionless. As for the woman, her eyes gleam, and her lips stretch into a malicious smile.

Woman: If it were possible for a man to force another to commit a serious crime merely by the power of suggestion, what great satisfaction he must derive. . . . Using an unsuspecting puppet to carry out his designs, he would be utterly safe from discovery. This, I think, is the perfect crime we never discussed.

Man: What—what the devil do you mean?

Woman: I'm only trying to tell you what kind of a man you really are! . . . But don't be alarmed. I have no intention of going screaming to the police. I'm quite an understanding woman, you know. Come now, let's not mince words.

Man: Listen, it's getting late—

Woman: See? I told you—you're afraid of me! But I simply hate to leave a story unfinished . . . so please let me continue. . . . To you, Saito was an ideal puppet. First, you awakened his interest in detective stories. Then you convinced him that the trick of the dual personality was foolproof. And, bit by bit, by the power of suggestion, you led him deeper and deeper into the pit of crime. . . . The fact that Saito had a mistress was a mere accident, but you used this too.

Man: You're crazy. . . . It's easy to put two and two together to fit any pattern. . . .

Woman: But think back. You know only too well that it was always you—and you alone—who made one event lead to the next—until I finally killed Saito. It was all your doing—by the sheer power of your suggestions—and you know it!

Man: But you've forgotten one thing. You might not have killed Saito!

Woman: In that case you would quickly have adopted some other strategy. Of all the kinds of criminals, you're the most cunning, for your strategy was based on probabilities. If one plan went wrong, you would quickly have thought up another . . . and another. . . . One of them was sure to succeed—and without your ever being suspected. Yes, you did indeed commit the perfect crime.

Man: You're beginning to annoy me. You've made up your story out of thin air, and it's sheer nonsense. I'm going back to the inn.

Woman: Look at you! Your face is covered with sweat. Don't tell me you're not feeling sick! But you'll have to hear me out. When I pulled the trigger of that pistol, I didn't see Saito holding any knife. I was only guessing that he was trying to kill me—so I killed him. . . . But I had another reason too. I loved you, and you knew it. . . . I didn't see the knife until after I'd recovered from the fainting spell—and there it lay beside Saito's body. Now, you were the first one to arrive on the scene after I killed Saito, and how utterly simple it would have been for you to put Saito's fingerprints on the knife and plant it beside his body. You thus not only got rid of Saito, but also provided evidence for my plea of self-defense.

Man: Your powers of imagination are truly amusing. Ha, ha.

Woman: You can't fool me with your laughter. Look, you're trembling! You needn't, you know. I'm not going to tell anyone. How could I betray you after you've gone to such great pains to get me? I only wanted to talk this over with you—just once. . . . I won't tell anyone, never fear.

The man rises silently from the bench, and the look he gives the girl eloquently states that he will have nothing more to do with a lunatic. The girl also gets to her feet, and ignoring the man, who stands still, she begins to walk slowly away toward the edge of the precipice. A moment later the man follows her.

Reaching a point only two feet away from the edge of the cliff, she stops. Far, far below, the faint sound of the flowing river rises above the mist that covers the chasm.

Without even turning her head, the girl continues to speak to the man behind her.

Woman: We've certainly bared our innermost thoughts today, haven't we? But there's one more thing I must tell you. I loved you only for yourself, but you loved my money as well as myself. And now, it's only my money you want. I know this. And you know I know it. Isn't it so? That's why you brought me to this lonely spot today. . . . Just like Saito, you can't live without my money, so you've begun to wish I'd have an accident. If something happened to me, of course, you would inherit all my money, because you are my husband. . . . I even happen to know that you too have a mistress—and that you hate me for being in the way.

At this point, the girl hears the man's heavy breathing behind her and knows that he has been gradually creeping closer and closer. She tells herself that the time had come. She feels his trembling hands suddenly grab her shoulders. They begin to push . . . harder . . . harder. At the precise moment when his hands shove for a final push, she jumps aside in a flash.

Losing his balance, the man staggers forward, clawing wildly at empty space. The next instant, his feet are treading thin air, and his body goes hurtling down into the yawning chasm.

Moments later, the merry chirping of birds is heard from amidst the surrounding foliage. In the distance the sinking sun is like a flaming ball, dyeing the hovering clouds a deep red.
The girl stands stock-still atop the cliff. Then, slowly and mechanically, she beings to mumble to herself.

Woman: Self-defense again. How funny! A year ago Saito tried to kill me. But he was the one who was killed, not I. And now that fool tried to push me off this cliff. But he was the one who fell off. . . . I was the real killer of both. But the law won't punish me. . . . How easy it is to kill! Who knows, maybe I really am the witch I seem . . . maybe I'm destined to go on forever, killing one husband after another. . . .

Like a lone pine, the girl continues to stand motionless on the edge of the cliff, gradually fading from view as darkness descends.

The
Hell of Mirrors

One of the strangest friends I ever had was Kan Tanuma. From the very start I suspected that he was mentally unbalanced. Some might have called him just eccentric, but I am convinced he was a lunatic. At any rate, he had one mania—a craze for anything capable of reflecting an image, as well as for all types of lenses. Even as a boy the only toys he would play with were magic lanterns, telescopes, magnifying glasses, kaleidoscopes, prisms, and the like.

Perhaps this strange mania of Tanuma's was hereditary, for his great-grandfather Moribe was also known to have had the same predilection. As evidence there is the collection of objects—primitive glassware and telescopes and ancient books on related subjects—which this Moribe obtained from the early Dutch merchants at Nagasaki. These were handed down to his descendants, and my friend Tanuma was the last in line to receive the heirlooms.

Although episodes concerning Tanuma's craze for mirrors and lenses in his boyhood are almost endless, those I remember most vividly took place in the latter part of his high-school days, when he was deeply involved in the study of physics, especially optics.

[Certain archaic terms have been amended. Ed.]

One day while we were in the classroom (Tanuma and I were classmates in the same school), the teacher passed around a concave mirror and invited all the students to observe the reflection of their faces in the glass. When my turn came to look I recoiled with horror, for the numerous festering pimples on my face, so greatly magnified, looked exactly like craters on the moon seen through the gigantic telescope of an astronomical observatory. I might mention that I had always been extremely sensitive about my heavily pimpled face, so much so that the shock I received on this occasion left me with a phobia of looking into such concave mirrors. On one occasion not long after this incident I happened to visit a science exhibition, but when I spotted an extra-large concave mirror mounted in the far distance I took to my heels in holy terror.

Tanuma, however, in sharp contrast to my sensitive feelings, let out a shrill cry of joy as soon as he got his first glance at that concave mirror in the classroom. "Wonderful . . . wonderful!" he shrieked, and all the other students laughed at him.

But to Tanuma the experience was no laughing matter, for he was in dead earnest. Subsequently his love for concave mirrors grew so intense that he was forever buying all sorts of paraphernalia—wire, cardboard, mirrors, and the like. From these he mischievously began constructing various devilish trick-boxes with the help of many books which he had procured, all devoted to the art of scientific magic.

Following Tanuma's graduation from high school, he showed no inclination to pursue his academic studies further. Instead, with the money which was generously supplied him by his easygoing parents, he built a small laboratory in one corner of his garden and devoted his full time and effort to his craze for optical instruments.

He completely isolated himself in his weird laboratory, and I was the only friend who ever visited him, the others having all given him up because of his growing eccentricity. On each of my visits I began to feel more and more anxious over his strange doings, for I could see clearly that his malady was going from bad to worse.

About this time both his parents died, leaving him with a handsome inheritance. Now completely free from any supervision, and with ample funds to satisfy his every whim, he began to grow more reckless than ever. At the same time, having now reached the age of twenty, he began to show a keen interest in the opposite sex. This interest intermingled with his morbid craze for optics, and the two grew into a powerful force in which he was completely enmeshed.

Immediately after receiving his inheritance he built a small observatory and equipped it with an astronomical telescope in order to explore the mysteries of the planets. As his house stood on a high elevation, it was an ideal spot for this purpose. But he was not one to be satisfied with such an innocuous occupation. Soon he began to turn his telescope earthward and to focus the lens on the houses of the surrounding area. Fences and other barriers constituted no obstacle, because his observatory stood on very high ground.

The occupants of the neighboring houses, utterly unaware of Tanuma's prying eyes peering through his telescope, went about their daily lives without any reserve, their sliding paper windows wide open. As a result Tanuma derived hitherto unknown pleasures from his secret explorations into the private lives of his neighbors. One evening he kindly invited me to take a look, but what I saw made me blush a deep crimson, and I refused to partake any more in his observations.

Not long after he built a special type of periscope which enabled him to get a full view of the rooms of his many young maidservants while he was sitting in his lab. Unaware of this, the maids showed no restraint in whatever they did in the privacy of their own rooms.

Another episode, which I can never erase from my mind, concerned insects. Tanuma began studying them under a small microscope, deriving childish delight from watching both their fighting and their mating. One particular scene which I had the misfortune of seeing was that of a crushed flea. This was a gory sight indeed, for, magnified a thousandfold, it looked like a large wild boar struggling in a pool of blood.

Some time after this, when I called on Tanuma one afternoon and knocked on his laboratory door, there was no answer. So I casually walked in, as was my custom. Inside, it was completely dark, for all the windows were draped with black curtains. And then suddenly on the large wall ahead of me there appeared some blurred and indescribable object, so monstrous in size that it covered the entire space. I was so startled that I stood transfixed.

Gradually the "thing" on the wall began to take definite shape. The first shape that came into focus was a swamp overgrown with black weeds. Beneath it there appeared two immense eyes the size of washtubs, with brown pupils glinting horribly, while at their sides there flowed many rivers of blood on a white plateau. Next came two large caves, from which there seemed to protrude the black bushy ends of large brooms. These, of course, were the hairs growing in the cavities of a gigantic nose. Then followed two thick lips, which looked like two large, crimson cushions; and they kept moving, exposing two rows of white teeth the proportions of roof-tiles.

It was a picture of a human face. Somehow I thought I recognized the features despite their grotesque size.

Just at this point I heard someone calling: "Don't be alarmed! It's only me!" The voice gave me another shock, for the large lips moved in synchronization with the words, and the eyes seemed to smile.

Abruptly, without any warning, the room was filled with light, and the apparition on the wall vanished. Almost simultaneously Tanuma emerged from behind a curtain at the rear of the room.

Grinning mischievously, he came up to me and exclaimed with childish pride: "Wasn't that a remarkable show?" While I continued to stand motionless, still speechless with wonder, he explained to me that what I had seen was an image of his own face, thrown on the wall by means of a stereopticon which he had had specially constructed to project the human face.

Several weeks later he started another new experiment. This time he built a small room within the laboratory, the interior of which was completely lined with mirrors. The four walls, plus floor and ceiling, were mirrors. Hence, anyone who went inside would be confronted with reflections of every portion of his body; and as the *six* mirrors reflected one another, the reflections multiplied and re-multiplied ad infinitum. Just what the purpose of the room was Tanuma never explained. But I do remember that he invited me on one occasion to enter it. I flatly refused, for I was terrified. But from what the servants told me Tanuma frequently entered the "chamber of mirrors" together with Kimiko, his favorite maid, a buxom girl of eighteen, to enjoy the hidden delights of mirrorland.

The servants also told me that at other times he would enter the chamber alone, staying for many minutes, often as long as an hour. Once he had stayed inside so long that the servants had become alarmed. One of them mustered up enough courage to knock on the door. Tanuma came leaping out, stark naked, and without even a word of explanation, fled to his own room.

I must explain at this juncture that Tanuma's health was fast deteriorating. On the other hand his craze for optical instruments kept increasing in intensity. Continuing to spend his fortune on his insane hobby, he kept laying in bigger and bigger stocks of mirrors of all shapes and descriptions—concave, convex, corrugated, prismatic—as well as miscellaneous specimens that cast completely distorted reflections. Finally,

127

however, he reached the stage where he could no longer find any further satisfaction unless he himself manufactured his own mirrors. So he established a glass-working plant in his spacious garden, and there, with the help of a select staff of technicians and workmen, began turning out all kinds of fantastic mirrors. He had no relative to restrain him in his insane ventures, and the handsome wages he paid his servants assured their complete obedience. Hence I felt it was my duty to try and dissuade him from squandering any more of his fast-dwindling fortune. But Tanuma would not listen to me.

I was nevertheless determined to keep an eye on him, fearing he might lose his mind completely, and visited him frequently. And on each occasion I was a witness to some still madder example of his mirror-making orgy, each example becoming more and more difficult to describe.

One of the things he did was to cover one whole wall of his laboratory with a giant mirror. Then in the mirror he cut out five holes; he would thrust his arms, legs, and head through these holes from the back side of the mirror, creating a weird illusion of a trunkless body floating in space.

On other occasions I would find his lab cluttered up with a miscellaneous collection of mirrors of fantastic shapes and sizes—corrugated, concave, and convex types predominating—and he would be dancing in their midst, completely naked, in the manner of some primitive pagan ritualist or witch doctor. Every time I beheld these scenes I got the shivers, for the reflection of his madly whirling naked body became contorted and twisted into a thousand variations. Sometimes his head would appear double, his lips swollen to immense proportions; again his belly would swell and rise, then flatten out; his swinging arms would multiply like those found on ancient Chinese Buddhist statues. Indeed, during such times the laboratory was transformed into a purgatory of freaks.

Next, Tanuma rigged up a gigantic kaleidoscope which seemed to fill the entire length of his laboratory. This was rotated by a motor, and with each rotation of the giant cylinder the mammoth flower patterns of the kaleidoscope would change in form and hue—red, pink, purple, green, vermilion, black—like the flowers of an opium addict's dream. And Tanuma himself would crawl into the cylinder, dancing there crazily among the flowers, his stark naked body and limbs multiplying like the petals of the flowers, making it seem as if he too were one of the flowery features of the kaleidoscope.

Nor did his madness end here—far from it. His fantastic creations multiplied rapidly, each on a larger scale than the previous one. Until about this time I had still believed that he was partly sane; but finally even I had to admit he had completely lost his mind. And shortly thereafter came the terrible, tragic climax.

One morning I was suddenly awakened by an excited messenger from Tanuma's house.

"A terrible thing has happened! Miss Kimiko wants you to come immediately!" the messenger cried, his face white as a sheet of rice-paper.

"What's the matter?" I asked, hurriedly getting into my clothes.

"We don't know yet," exclaimed the servant. "But for God's sake, come with me at once!"

I tried to question the servant further, but he was so incoherent that I gave up and hurried as fast as I could to Tanuma's laboratory.

Entering that eerie place, the first person I saw was Kimiko, the attractive young parlormaid whom Tanuma had made his mistress. Near her stood several of the other maids, all huddled together and gazing horror-struck at a large spherical object reposing in the center of the room.

This sphere was about twice as large as the ball on which circus clowns often balance themselves. The exterior was completely covered with white cloth. What terrified me was the fantastic way this sphere kept rolling slowly and haphazardly, as if it were alive. Far more terrible, however, was the strange noise that echoed faintly from the interior of the ball—it was a laugh, a spine-chilling laugh that seemed to come from the throat of a creature from some other world.

"What—what's going on? What in the world is happening?" I asked the stunned group.

"We—we don't know," one of the maids replied dazedly. "We think our master's inside. But we can't do anything. We've called several times, but there's been no answer except the weird laughter you hear now."

Hearing this, I approached the sphere gingerly, trying to find out how the sounds got out of the sphere. Soon I discovered several small air holes. Pressing my eye to one of these small openings, I peered inside; but I was blinded by a brilliant light and could see nothing clearly. However, I *did* ascertain one thing—there was a creature inside!

"Tanuma! Tanuma!" I called out several times, putting my mouth against the hole. But the same weird laughter was all that I could hear.

Not knowing what to do next, I stood, uncertainly watching the ball roll about. And then suddenly I noticed the thin lines of a square partition on the smooth exterior surface. I realized at once that this was a door, allowing entry into the sphere. "But if it's a door, where's the knob?" I asked myself. Examining the door carefully, I saw a small screw-hole which must have held some kind of a handle.

At the sight of this I was struck by a terrible thought. "It's quite possible," I told myself, "that the handle has accidentally come loose, trapping inside whoever it is that entered the sphere. If so, the man must have spent the entire night inside, unable to get out."

Searching the floor of the laboratory, I soon found a T-shaped handle. I tried to fit it to the hole, but it would not work, for the stem was broken.

I could not understand why in the world the man inside—if indeed it was a man—didn't shout and scream for help instead of letting out those weird chuckles and laughs. "Maybe," I suddenly reminded myself with a start, "Tanuma is inside and has gone stark raving mad."

I quickly decided that there was but one thing to do. I hurried to the glass works, picked up a heavy hammer, and rushed back into the lab. Aiming carefully, I brought the hammer down on the globe with all my might. Again and again I struck at the strange object, and it was soon reduced to a mass of thick fragments of glass.

The man who crawled out of the debris was indeed none other than Tanuma. But he was almost unrecognizable, for he had undergone a horrible transformation. His face was pulpy and discolored; his eyes kept wandering aimlessly; his hair was a shaggy tangle; his mouth was agape, the saliva dripping down in thin, foamy ribbons. His entire expression was that of a raving maniac.

Even the girl Kimiko recoiled with horror after taking one glance at this monstrosity of a man. Needless to say, Tanuma had gone completely insane.

"But how did this come about?" I asked myself. "Could the mere fact of confinement inside this glass sphere have been enough to drive him mad? Moreover, what was his motive in constructing the globe in the first place?"

Although I questioned the servants still huddled close to me, I could learn nothing, for they all swore they had known nothing of the globe, not even that it had existed.

As though completely oblivious of his whereabouts, Tanuma began to wander about the room, still grinning. Kimiko overcame her initial fright with great effort and tearfully tugged at his sleeves. Just at this moment the chief engineer of the glass works arrived on the scene to report for work.

Ignoring his shock at what he saw, I started to fire questions at him relentlessly. The man was so bewildered that he could barely stammer out his replies. But this is what he told me:

A long time ago Tanuma had ordered him to construct this glass sphere. Its walls were half an inch thick and its diameter about four feet. In order to make the interior a one-unit mirror, Tanuma had the workmen and engineers paint the exterior of the globe with quicksilver, over which they pasted several layers of cotton cloth. The interior of the globe had been built in such a way that there were small cavities here and there as receptacles for electric bulbs which would not protrude. Another feature of the globe was a door just large enough to permit the entrance of an average-sized man.

The engineers and workers had been completely unaware of the purpose of the product, but orders were orders, and so they had gone ahead with their assignment. At last, on the night before, the globe had been finished, complete with an extra-long electric cord fitted to a socket on the outer surface, and it had been carefully brought into the lab. They plugged the cord into a wall socket, and then departed at once, leaving Tanuma alone with the sphere. What happened later was, of course, beyond the realm of their knowledge.

After hearing the chief engineer's story, I asked him to leave. Then, putting Tanuma in the custody of the servants, who led him away to the house proper, I continued to stand alone in the laboratory, my eyes fixed on the glass fragments scattered about the room, desperately trying to solve the mystery of what had happened.

For a long while I stood thus, wrestling with the conundrum. Finally I reached the conclusion that Tanuma, after having completely exhausted every new idea in his mania of optics, had decided that he would construct a glass globe, completely lined with a single-unit mirror, which he would enter in order to see his own reflection.

Why would a man become crazy if he entered a glass globe lined with a mirror? What in the name of the devil had he seen there? When these thoughts passed through my mind, I felt as if I had been stabbed through the spine with a sword of ice.

Did he go mad after taking a glance at himself reflected by a completely spherical mirror? Or did he slowly lose his sanity after suddenly discovering that he was trapped inside his horrible round glass coffin—together with "that" reflection?

What, then, I asked myself again, had he seen? It was surely something completely beyond the scope of human imagination. Assuredly, never before had anyone shut himself up within the confines of a mirror-lined sphere. Even a trained physicist could not have guessed exactly what sort of vision would be created inside that sphere. Probably it would be a thing so unthinkable as to be utterly out of this world of ours.

So strange and terrifying must have been this reflection, of whatever shape it was, as it filled Tanuma's complete range of vision, that it would have made any mortal insane.

The only thing we know is the reflection cast by a concave mirror, which is only one section of a spherical whole. It is a monstrously huge magnification. But who could possibly imagine what the result would be when one is wrapped up in a complete succession of concave mirrors?

My hapless friend, undoubtedly, had tried to explore the regions of the unknown, violating sacred taboos, thereby incurring the wrath of the gods. By trying to pry open the secret portals of forbidden knowledge with his weird mania of optics he had destroyed himself.

The Twins

[A CONDEMNED CRIMINAL'S
CONFESSION TO A PRIEST]

Father, I've finally made up my mind to confess to you. My day of execution is drawing nearer; and I want to make a clean breast of all my sins, for I feel that this is the only way I can obtain a few days of peace before I die. So I beg you to spare me some of your valuable time to hear the story of my wicked life.

As you know, I've been sentenced to death for the crime of killing a man and stealing two million yen from his safe. I did in fact commit that crime, but no one suspects me of anything more than that. So, now that I am destined to face my Maker, there is no reason on earth why I should confess to another crime far more diabolical. But my heart is set on confessing all while there is yet time; after I have paid the supreme penalty, my lips will be sealed forever.

After you've heard my confession, Father, I beseech you to tell my wife everything, for it is only right that she should know too. The greatest of scoundrels often turn out to be good men when death is near at hand. I think my wife would hate me forever if I were to die without confessing to the *other crime* as well. And there's yet one more reason. I've always had a livid fear of the vengeance of the man I murdered! No, I don't

[Certain archaic terms have been amended. Ed.]

mean the one I killed when I stole the money. That case is already closed, for I have already confessed my guilt. The fact is, I committed another murder before that. And whenever I think of my first victim I almost go mad with terror.

The first man I sent to his grave was my elder brother—but he was no ordinary brother. We were twins, born from our mother's womb almost simultaneously.

Although he has long been dead, he haunts me day and night. In my dreams he treads on my chest with the weight of a thousand pounds; and then he clutches me by the throat and chokes me. In the daytime he appears on the wall there and stares at me with ghastly eyes, or shows his face in that window and laughs at me grimly. And the fact that we were twins, identical to each other in looks, in the shapes of our bodies, in everything, made things all the worse. No sooner had I killed him than he began to appear before me every time I looked at myself. When I think about the past it seems to me that it was my brother's desire for revenge that made me commit the second murder, which led to my ultimate undoing.

From the moment I cut off my twin's life, I began to fear all mirrors. In fact, not only mirrors, but everything that reflected. I removed every mirror and all the glassware in my house. But what was the use? All the shops on the streets had show windows, and behind them, more mirrors glittered. The more I tried not to look at them, the more my eyes were attracted to them. And, wherever I gazed, his face—his mad, leering face—stared back at me, full of vengeance; it was, of course, my own face.

Once in front of a mirror-shop I almost fainted, for there I was set upon not just by one face of the man I had killed, but by thousands of his faces, with a number of eyes that seemed incredible.

Although I was greatly dismayed by such illusions, my spirit did not break; I was reassured and emboldened by the firm belief that the scheme which I had concocted in this clever head of mine could never be exposed. And the constant strain on my mind, making it necessary for me to be perpetually on the alert and never to relax even for a fleeting moment, gave me no time to be afraid. But, now that I am a prisoner, my mind is too weak to resist, and his ghost, taking advantage of my monotonous life in prison, has gained complete possession of my senses. Thus ever since being condemned to the gallows, I have been living in a perpetual nightmare.

Although there is no mirror in this jail, he appears in the reflection of my face in the water when I wash or take a bath. Even the surfaces of tableware, glistening hardware, and, in fact, anything that reflects light, gives back to me the sight of his image, now large, now small. Even my shadow cast by the sunlight from that window there scares me. And, worst of all, I dread seeing my own body, for it, too, is an exact replica of that of my dead brother, down to the faintest wrinkle.

I would rather die than continue to be kept in this agony— a hell on earth. Instead of fearing my execution, I look forward to it, and the sooner it takes place the better. But at the same time I feel that I simply cannot die without first telling the truth. I must get his forgiveness before I die, but if not that, I would at least like to drive away the feeling of being haunted. I know of only one way to achieve this. It is to confess my crime.

Father, please listen closely to my confession, and later please tell the court as well as my wife. I know it is much to ask of you, but I have only a little longer to live, and it is my sole request. And now I'll tell you about my other crime.

First let me repeat that I was born as one of a pair of twins so strangely identical, so completely the same that it seemed as if we had been cast in the same mold. There was, however, a single distinguishing feature. This was a mole on my thigh, the one sign that made it possible for our parents to tell us apart. If our hairs had been counted, I would not have been surprised had the number been the same. This very singular similarity between us was, I now believe, the seed which gradually took root in my mind, tempting me to kill my other half.

When I finally decided to kill my brother I really had no special reason to be bitter towards him other than that of a burning jealousy on my part. The fact of the matter was that he inherited an immense fortune as first-born son and heir, while my share was incomparably smaller. At the same time, the woman whom I had loved became his wife; her parents had forced her to marry him because of his superiority over me in fortune and position. Naturally, this was our parents' fault rather than his. If I wanted to hate, I should have become bitter against my deceased parents rather than against my brother. Besides, he was innocent of the knowledge that his wife had once been my heart's desire. But hate him I did— with all my soul.

So, if I had been capable of thinking rationally, nothing would have happened. But, unfortunately, I was born wicked, and I didn't know how to get on in the world. And to make matters worse, I had no definite aim in life, being a confirmed wastrel. I had become the kind of rogue who is satisfied only with living a life of idleness, living from day to day without a thought for tomorrow. Therefore, after losing both my fortune and my love at one stroke, I suppose I became desperate. At any rate, I immediately squandered foolishly the money I received as my share.

Consequently, there was nothing for me to do but to appeal to him for financial help. And I used to give him a great deal of trouble. He gradually became annoyed at my repeated calls for help, and one day he told me flatly that he would put a halt to his generosity unless I mended my ways.

One afternoon, on my way home from his house after having been refused another loan, a terrible idea suddenly occurred to me. When I first thought of it, I trembled with fear and tried to shake it off. But the idea kept coming back like a persistent melody, and the more I turned it over in my mind the more I decided it was quite a feasible plot. I gradually came to think that here was the opportunity of a lifetime, that if I carried out my scheme cleverly and resolutely, I could obtain both fortune and love without any danger. For several days I thought of nothing except my sinister plan. And after considering every possible angle, I finally decided the coast was absolutely clear and I could go ahead.

Please believe that my wicked resolution did not grow out of any feelings of animosity. As a born rogue, I only wanted to obtain pleasure at any cost. But in spite of my wicked nature, I was still a coward and would never have made such a resolution had I anticipated the slightest danger. But there was not the faintest chance of failure—or at least so I believed.

I quickly began to put my plans into operation. First, as a preliminary step, I visited his house more frequently and studied his and his wife's daily behavior closely. Painstakingly, I tried to observe and to remember every detail of their lives, overlooking nothing. For instance, I even went to the extent of noting the way he wrung his towel after washing.

After about a month, when I had completed all my observations, I suddenly announced without any warning that I was all set to go to Korea to find work. At the time I was still a confirmed bachelor, so my sudden announcement did not arouse any suspicion. On the contrary, my brother rejoiced when he heard the news, although I had a sneaking suspicion that he was jubilant only because he thought he was finally to be rid of me. At any rate, he gave me a considerable sum of money as a farewell gift.

One day soon after—it was a day which suited all my plans perfectly—I boarded a Shimonoseki-bound train at Tokyo Station and waved farewell to my brother and his wife. But after only an hour or so I stole off the train at Yamakita and, after waiting some time, took a train back to Tokyo. Traveling by third class and mingling with the crowd, I was soon back in Tokyo without anyone's knowing.

I should explain at this point that while I waited for the Tokyo train at Yamakita Station, I went into the restroom and cut out the mole on my thigh with a razor—the one and only mark which distinguished me from my brother. After this simple operation, my brother and I were carbon copies, so to speak.

When I arrived at Tokyo, dawn was just breaking. This too was part of my plan. Without losing any time, I quickly changed into a kimono I had had made for the purpose before starting out; it was of the same Oshima silk which my brother used for everyday wear. Furthermore, I also put on the same kind of underwear, wore the same sash, the same clogs, in fact, everything that he usually wore. Then I went to his house at the right time, carefully figured out to a split second. Taking extra care that nobody should see me, I climbed over the back fence and stole into his spacious garden.

It was still very early in the morning and dark, so no one noticed me as I crept up to the side of the well in one corner of the garden. This old abandoned well was one of the most important factors which prompted me to commit the crime. It had run dry long ago, and had not been used since. I remembered my brother's having said at one time that it was dangerous to have such a trap in the garden and that he intended to fill it up soon. A mound of earth was now piled up high beside the well, no doubt having been brought there by the gardeners, to whom I had suggested only a few days ago that they fill up the hole on this very day.

I crouched down, hiding myself in the shrubbery, and waited calmly, expecting at any moment to hear my brother's footsteps, for it was his custom to take a stroll in the garden every morning after his toilet. As I waited, I felt cold beads of sweat run down along my arms from my armpits. How long I waited I do not recall, except that time seemed to stand completely still. Perhaps it was about three hours later—hours which seemed more like years—when I at last heard the clatter of his clogs. My first impulse was to run away—to escape from the horror of my own devilish scheme; but somehow my legs seemed to have grown roots in the ground, and I couldn't move.

Before I knew it, my long-awaited victim had arrived just in front of the shrubbery in which I was concealed, and I realized with a start that my time had come. With amazing agility, I suddenly sprang out and wound the rope which I had prepared around my brother's neck—and then I slowly proceeded to strangle him.

Desperately he struggled, twisting and squirming, and frequently he tried to look back to see who his assailant was. I in turn tried with all my might to keep him from doing so. But his discolored face, as though it was being worked by a very strong spring, slowly turned back toward me, inch by inch. Finally, his red, swollen face—it was just the same as mine—turned back and came into range, and from the corners of his mad, staring eyes, he beheld my face. As soon as he recognized me, he shuddered, as if from shock. Never will I be able to forget his face at that moment. It was a death mask, a horrible countenance which cried out for vengeance!

Soon, however, he ceased to struggle. Then he turned limp and fell to the ground. By this time I was exhausted, and after I dropped him, I rubbed my hands vigorously because they were rigid and paralyzed from the strain. Then, my knees still knocking together, I rolled his dead body like a log to the well opening and pushed it in headfirst. Next, I picked up a board and used it to scoop enough of the loose dirt into the well to cover the corpse.

Had there been a witness to the scene, he would certainly have thought it nothing but a bad nightmare. Just imagine!—

he would have seen one man strangling another wearing the same clothes, possessing the same figure and even the same face.

Well, thus it was that I committed the great crime of killing my own brother. It was the same story as that of Cain and his brother Abel, only in our case the brothers looked exactly alike, for did we not share identical bodies?

Does it surprise you that anyone could perpetrate such a cold-blooded crime? I do not wonder. But as for me, the very reason for my wanting to kill him was that we were two persons in one. And how I *hated* my other half! I wonder whether you've ever had such a feeling of uncontrollable hatred, far more severe than that which you could feel against any person not closely related to you. And in my particular case it was still more so because we were twins and I was insane with jealousy.

To continue with my story, after I covered the body with enough earth, I still lingered on, absorbed in contemplation. After about half an hour I suddenly noticed with alarm that the gardeners were coming, led by a maid, and I again concealed myself. Immediately the devil in me again whispered that this was the cue for my second entrance on the stage for a brutally deceptive play—a performance starring a maniac!

Impersonating my brother, I calmly came out of hiding and turned my face toward them a little nervously.

"Well, well," I said as naturally as possible, "so you've come early. I've helped you with your work a little, ha-ha. I hope you can fill up the well by nightfall. Well, you'd better get started!"

With these words, I slowly walked away with the familiar gait of my dead brother and went into the house.

After that everything went like clockwork. I kept to the study all that day, my nose buried in my brother's diary and account books, for although I had studied everything else before announcing that I was going to Korea, I had been unable to get at these two items. In the evening I sat at the dining table

with my "wife"—the woman who had been my brother's wife and who now was mine—chatting pleasantly in the same way my brother had done, conscious that she was utterly unaware of the horrible truth.

Late that night I even ventured into her bedroom, but once there, I felt a little shaky, for I hadn't the faintest notion about his habits in this private chamber. However, still bubbling over with self-confidence—it was my firm belief that even if she did find out the truth, she would not spurn me, her old sweet-heart—I opened the sliding door of her boudoir composedly and soon switched off the lights.

Once I had gone so far as to commit adultery as well as murder, my mind was now at rest, and I continued to live happily for a year. With plenty of money to spend, and with the woman I had once loved at my beck and call, my life seemed one of perpetual bliss—but there was one hitch—my conscience. Night after night it tormented me, while his apparition haunted my dreams. In fact, this period of a year was the longest I had ever experienced. Gradually, like the complete rogue that I was, I began to grow weary of my humdrum life.

Again, I fell into my old bad habits. My brother's large fortune soon began to dwindle, as I spent money like water, and I discovered one day that instead of being a rich man I was up to my neck in debt. Furthermore, I no longer had anyone to turn to. What a curse! This was what spurred me on to commit the second crime.

If you reflect carefully, you'll see that this was but a natural sequence to my first murder. When I first decided to kill my brother I already had this second plot in the making. I had decided that if I could manage to become my elder brother in every minute detail, nothing would stand in the way of my committing other crimes. You see, even if the younger brother, about whom nothing whatever had been heard after his departure for Korea, committed a murder or burglary or any other crime, the elder brother would always be free from blame or suspicion.

Also, there was another peculiar circumstance in this singular chain of events. After my first crime I chanced upon a surprising discovery, one which showed me how easy it would be to commit my next crime without any danger of detection.

One day I was making an entry for the day in his diary, copying his handwriting carefully. This was really a nuisance, but it had to be done, for it had been another of his daily habits. After writing a few lines, I compared the part written by me with a part written by him, and I was startled to find a fingerprint on one corner of the page; evidently it was my brother's.

For a moment the shock of the discovery stunned me, for I had overlooked this most important detail. Carelessly I had thought all along that the mole on my thigh was the only difference between my brother and me, and now I was stumped. What a fool I had been! Why, even a grade school student knows that every person in the world has his own type of fingerprints, and I, of all people, should have known that even twins never have identical fingerprints! Now, at the sight of his fingerprint in the diary I was overcome by the fear that it might betray me.

Secretly I bought a magnifying glass and studied the smudge, which turned out to be a thumbprint. I stamped my own thumbprint on a piece of paper and compared the two. Upon casual observation, the two prints seemed very similar. But then I examined them closely, line by line, coil by coil, and detected many differences. I next secretly took the fingerprints of my "wife" and the maids for caution's sake, but they were so different that I didn't even need to compare them with the one in the diary. Assuredly, the one in the book was my brother's thumbprint. Since we were twins, it was natural that it resembled my own.

Thinking it would be a serious matter if any other fingerprints of this sort existed, I made an exhaustive search for more. I examined all the books, page by page, looked in the dust in every corner of the shelves, in the closets, the ward-robe, in fact in every conceivable place where his fingerprints might have been left. But I could find no others. This relieved me somewhat, but I was taking no chances. Quickly I tore the page out of the diary and was about to throw it into the char-coal brazier, thinking that if this single piece of evidence was destroyed, I would have nothing further to worry about. But then a bright idea suddenly struck me. It seemed to come like an inspiration—not from any angel but from the devil himself.

Wouldn't it be very handy, I told myself, if I could make a cast of the thumbprint. Why, I could plant it on the scene of my next crime . . . and the ones after that. No one could re-member the fingerprints of my actual self, so no one could tell whose they were . . . and the very fact that my own fingerprints would not match those of my brother's would establish my in-nocence. As for the police, they would have to search for the person who bore the fingerprints, not knowing that he was buried a good thirty feet under the ground.

This wonderful idea raised me to a seventh heaven of de-light. Why, I would be able to play the fantastic role of Dr. Je-kyll and Mr. Hyde in reality—and never be caught.

Putting my wicked plot into operation, I soon stole a large sum of money from the house of a friend and purposely left my brother's thumbprint. This was easy, for I once had some ex-perience as a photoengraver, and of course I had made a block.

After this, whenever I was short of money for my merry-making, I resorted to this means, and was never once suspected or apprehended. Intoxicated by my success, I continued to steal right and left, and as the law never seemed to catch up with me, I finally went to the extent of committing another murder.

Of this last crime of mine you must have read the records, so I'll not go into too much detail. Suffice it to say that I learned of a large sum of money in the possession of another friend—

two million yen to be exact, reposing in his safe. When I further learned that the money was kept secretly as campaign funds for a political campaign, the setup seemed just about perfect.

After studying every detail, I stole into his house one night as my natural self—the younger brother. Creeping into the room where the money was kept, I opened the door of the safe with gloved hands and took out the bundles of banknotes. (I knew the combination because he had once opened the safe in my presence, trusting me because I—that is to say, my dead brother—was an old acquaintance.)

Suddenly the lights I had extinguished were turned on. Startled, I turned around and found the owner of the safe confronting me! Desperately, I snatched a knife out of my pocket and stabbed him in the chest. Groaning, he sank to the floor and, in a few moments, was dead. I strained my ears, but fortunately no one had been aroused by the sound of the brief struggle.

After recovering my breath, I took out the engraved thumbprint of my brother and dipped it in the blood that had been spilt on the floor. I then stamped it on the wall nearby, and after making sure that there was no other evidence, I ran away at top speed, taking every precaution against leaving any footprints.

On the following day, a detective paid me a visit. But this did not disturb me at all, for I was still confident that the trick would work again. He told me apologetically and politely that he had visited every person who must have known of the large sum of money in the safe of the victim. Furthermore, he said that a thumbprint had been left on the spot, that it had not matched that of any ex-convict, and that he was sorry to trouble me but he wanted me to let him have my thumbprint as I had also known of the money in the safe. "Merely a matter of routine," he assured me.

Laughing at him inwardly, I asked many questions as if to show that I grieved the loss of my friend, and then let him take my thumbprint. After the detective left, I immediately forgot all about him and hurried to my favorite merrymaking hang-out with a well-filled purse.

Two or three days later the same detective paid me another visit. I found out later that he was a crack sleuth of the Metropolitan Police Board. When I casually walked into the drawing room, the detective looked at me with a peculiar smile. The next moment my head was swimming . . . swimming in a whirlpool of despair. Calmly, the man had placed a sheet of paper on the table, and when I looked, I saw what it was—a warrant for my arrest!

While I gazed at the paper, almost hypnotized with terror, he approached me quickly and handcuffed me. The next moment I noticed that a burly policeman had been waiting outside the door.

Shortly after, I was behind iron bars. However, I was naive enough to believe that I still had a chance. I was confident that they could never prove that I had committed the murder. But what a surprise awaited me! When I appeared before the procurator and heard his summation of the charges against me, I was pinned to the floor in open-mouthed amazement. I, who had always been so clever, had made such an absurd mistake that I was almost tempted to laugh out in self-mockery. Surely, this must have been my brother's curse!

How had I erred? Really, it was too foolish for words. The thumbprint which I had believed to have been my brother's was actually mine! The mark I had found in the diary was not a direct fingerprint but had been pressed there after I had once wiped my ink-stained fingers off. So it was the ink which remained in the shallow grooves between the ridges rather than the ridges themselves which had made the mark, producing a print like the negative of a photograph.

It had been such a careless mistake that I could hardly believe it was true. The procurator voluntarily told me of a case that had happened in 1913. He said that the wife of a merchant in Fukuoka was wantonly killed one day and that the police arrested a suspect. The fingerprint left on the scene of the crime and that of the suspect didn't seem to tally, although they looked very much alike. After being put off the scent completely, the police asked a specialist to study the prints scientifically, and at length, they were proved to be identical. The case had been the same as mine. The fingerprint on the spot had been the negative. But the expert, after close investigation, had reversed one of the photographs of the two fingerprints, changing the black to white—and the photographs then matched perfectly, thus proving the case. Now I have told you everything. I beg you, Father, to make the facts known, especially to my "wife," for only then will I be able to climb the thirteen steps to the scaffold on steady feet.

The Red Chamber

he seven grave men, including myself, had gathered as usual to exchange bloodcurdling horror stories. We sank into the deep armchairs, covered with scarlet velvet, in the room which had been dubbed the "Red Chamber" and waited eagerly for the narrator of the evening to begin his tale.

In the center of the group was a large, round table, also covered with scarlet velvet, and on it was a carved bronze candelabrum in which three large candles burned with flickering flames. On all sides of the room—even over the doors and windows—heavy red-silk curtains hung in graceful folds from ceiling to floor. The flames of the candles cast monstrously enlarged shadows of the secret society of seven on the curtains in hues dark like that of blood. Rising and falling, expanding and contracting, the seven silhouettes crept among the curves of the crimson drapery like horrible insects.

In this chamber I always felt as though I were sitting in the belly of some enormous, prehistoric beast, and thought I could even feel its heart beat in a slow tempo appropriate to its hugeness.

[Certain archaic terms have been amended. Ed.]

For a while all of us remained silent. As I sat with the rest like one bewitched, I unconsciously stared at the dark-red shadowy faces around the table and shuddered. Although I was perfectly familiar with the features of the others, I always felt chills creep down my spine whenever I studied them at close hand, for they all seemed perpetually unexpressive and motionless, like Japanese *Noh* masks.

At last, Tanaka, who had only recently been initiated into the society, cleared his throat to speak. He sat poised on the edge of his chair, gazing at the candle flames. I happened to glance at his chin, but what I saw seemed more like a square block of bone—without flesh or skin—and his whole face was akin to that of an ugly marionette strangely come alive.

"Having been admitted to the society as an accredited member," Tanaka suddenly began without any introduction, "I shall now proceed to contribute my first tale of horror."

As none of us made any move or comment, he quickly launched forth into his narrative:

I believe [he said] that I am in my right mind and that all my friends will vouch for my sanity, but whether I am really mentally fit or not, I will leave to you to judge. Yes, I may be mad! Or perhaps I may just be a mild neurotic case. But, at any rate, I must explain that I have always been weary of life . . . and to me the normal man's daily routine is—and always will be—a hateful boredom.

At first I gave myself up to various dissipations to distract my mind, but unfortunately, nothing seemed to relieve my profound boredom. Instead, everything I did only seemed to increase my disappointment the more. Constantly I kept asking myself: Is there no amusement left in the world for me? Am I doomed to die of yawning? Gradually I fell into a state of lethargy from which there seemed to be no escape. Nothing that I did—absolutely nothing—succeeded in pleasing my fancy. Every day I took three meals, and when the evening shadows fell I went to bed. Slowly I began to feel that I was going stark raving mad. Eating and sleeping, eating and sleeping—just like a hog.

If my circumstances had required that I hustle for my daily living, perhaps my constant boredom would have been relieved. But such was not my luck. By this I do not mean to imply that I was born fabulously rich. If this had been the case, then again there might have been a solution to my problem, for certainly money would have brought me thrills in plenty—orgies in luxurious living, eccentric debaucheries, or even bloody sports as in the days of Nero and the gladiators—so long as I could pay the price. But, curse my luck, I was neither destitute nor rich, just comfortably well-off, with funds sufficient to ensure only an average standard of living.

To any ordinary audience I would at this point enlarge upon the tortures of a life of boredom. But to you gentlemen of the Red Chamber Society I know this is unnecessary. Assuredly it was for the very purpose of banishing the specter of boredom that has haunted you, as it has me, that you formed this society. Therefore I will not digress but continue with my story.

At all times, as I have stated, I wrestled with the all-absorbing question: How am I to amuse myself? On some occasions I toyed with the idea of becoming a detective and finding amusement in tracking down criminals. At other times I pondered the possibilities of psychic experiments, or even of eroticism. How about producing obscene motion pictures? Or better still, how about private pornographic stage productions with prostitutes and sexual maniacs for the cast? Other ideas which occurred to me were visits to lunatic asylums and prisons or, if permission could be gotten, the witnessing of executions. But for one reason or another none of these ideas appealed to me very strongly. To put it another way they seemed like a soft drink offered to a dipsomaniac who is thirsting for gin and absinthe, cognac and vodka, all in one glass. Yes, that was what I needed—a good stiff drink of amusement—real soul-satisfying amusement.

Suddenly, just when I was about to conclude that I would never find a solution to my problem, an idea struck me—a horrible idea. At first I tried to shake it from me, for indeed my mind was now wading through treacherous swamps, and I knew I would be doomed if I did not check my impulses. And yet, the idea seemed to hold for me a peculiar fascination which I had never hitherto experienced. In short, gentlemen, the idea was . . . murder! Yes, here at last was an idea that seemed more worthy of a man of my character, a man willing to go to any lengths for a real thrill.

Finally, after convincing myself that I would never find peace of mind until I had committed a few murders, I carefully began to put some devilish plans into operation, just for the sheer pleasure of satisfying my lust for distraction. And now, at this point, before I proceed further, permit me to confess that, since that day when I first decided to become a murderer, I have been responsible for the deaths of nearly a hundred men, women, and children! Yes, almost a hundred innocent lives sacrificed on the altar of my eccentricity!

You might have inferred that I am now repentant for all the ghastly crimes I have committed. Well, that is definitely not the case. To tell the truth, I am not penitent at all. Far from it, for the fact of the matter is I have no conscience! So, instead of being racked with remorse, as apparently would any normal person, I simply became tired even of the bloody stimulus of murder. Again seeking some new diversion, I next took up the vice of opium-smoking. Gradually I became addicted to the drug, and today I can no longer do without a pipe at regular intervals.

So far, gentlemen, I have merely outlined the circumstances of my past—the murder of nearly a hundred people, all as yet undetected. I know, however, that the Supreme Judge who will pass sentence upon me for all my crimes is already demanding that I enter the portals of eternity, to roast in hellfire.

Now I shall relate the various events that made up my premeditated festival of crime. I do not doubt even for a moment that, when you have heard all the gruesome details, you will consider me a worthy member of your mystic society!

It all began about three years ago. In those days, as I have already told you, I was tired of every normal pastime and idled away my time with nothing whatever to do. In the spring of the year—as it was still very cold, it must have been about the end of February or the beginning of March—I had a strange experience one evening, the very incident that led me to take nearly one hundred lives.

I had been out late somewhere and, if I remember correctly, was a little tipsy. The time was about one in the morning. As I walked at a leisurely pace toward home, I suddenly came upon a man who seemed to be in a state of great confusion. I was startled when we almost collided, but he seemed to be even more frightened, for he stopped in his tracks, trembling. After a moment he peered into my face in the dim light of a street lamp and, to my great surprise, suddenly spoke.

"Does any doctor live hereabouts?" he asked.

"Yes," I immediately replied and asked what had happened.

The man hastily explained that he was a chauffeur and that he had accidentally run down and injured an old man who appeared to be a vagrant, some distance down the road. When he pointed out where the accident had occurred, I realized that it was in the very neighborhood of my house.

"Go to the left for a couple of blocks," I directed, "and you will find a house with a red lamp on the left-hand side. That's the office of Dr. Matsui. You'd better go there."

A few moments later I saw the chauffeur carrying the badly injured man to the house I had indicated. For some reason I kept watching until their dim figures vanished into the darkness. As I thought it inadvisable to interfere in such an affair, I returned to my bachelor quarters and promptly sank into the bed which had been prepared by my old housekeeper. Soon the alcohol in my system had me deep in sleep.

If, with the coming of sleep, I had forgotten all about that accident, it would have been the end of the affair. When I woke up the next morning, however, I remembered every detail of the previous night's episode. I began to wonder if the man who had been run down had succumbed to his injuries or had survived. Then suddenly something came to my mind with a jolt. Due to some strange quirk of the mind, or possibly because of the wine I had drunk, I had made a serious error in the directions I had given the chauffeur.

I was amazed. However drunk I might have been, I had surely not been out of my mind. Then why had I instructed the driver of the car to carry the unconscious man to the office of Dr. Matsui?

"Go to the left for a couple of blocks and you'll find a house with a red lamp on the left-hand side. . . ." I remembered every word I had uttered. Why, why, hadn't I instructed the man to go to the right for one block and seek the aid of Dr. Kato, a well-known surgeon? Matsui, the doctor whom I had recommended to the chauffeur, was a notorious quack, utterly without experience in surgery. On the other hand, Dr. Kato was a brilliant surgeon. As I had known this all along, how, I kept asking myself, had I ever come to make such a silly mistake?

I began to feel more and more anxious over my blunder and sent my old housekeeper to make a few discreet inquiries among the neighbors. When she returned from her mission I learned that the worst had happened. Dr. Matsui had failed miserably in his surgical efforts, and the victim of the accident had died without recovering consciousness. According to the gossip of the neighbors, when the injured man was carried into the office of Dr. Matsui, the latter made no mention of the fact that he was a novice in surgery. If, even at that eleventh hour, he had directed the chauffeur to take the man to Dr. Kato, the unfortunate man might still have been saved. But, no! Rashly, he had worked on the man himself, and had failed.

When I learned these tragic facts, all my blood seemed to drain out of my body. Who had actually been responsible for the death of the poor old man, I asked myself. Of course, the chauffeur and Dr. Matsui had their share of the responsibility. And if someone had to be punished, the guardians of the law would certainly pick the chauffeur. And yet, wasn't it *I* who had really been the most responsible? If I had not made the fatal error of indicating the wrong doctor, that old man might have been saved! The chauffeur had only injured the victim . . . he had not killed him outright. As for Dr. Matsui, his failure was attributable only to his lack of surgical skill, and to no other cause. But I—I had been criminally negligent and had pronounced the death sentence on an innocent man.

Actually, of course, I was innocent, for I had only committed a blunder. But then, I asked myself, what if I had *purposely* given the wrong directions? Needless to say, in that case I would have been guilty of murder! And yet, even if the law were to punish the chauffeur, not the slightest suspicion would have fallen on me—the real murderer! Besides, even if I had been suspected in some way, could they have hanged me if I had testified in court that because I had been in a state of intoxication I had forgotten all about Dr. Kato, the good surgeon? All these thoughts raised a fascinating problem.

Gentlemen, have you ever theorized on murder along these lines? I myself thought of it for the first time only after the experience I have just related. If you ponder deeply on the matter, you will find that the world is indeed a dangerous place. Who knows when you yourselves may be directed to the wrong doctor—*intentionally, criminally*—by a man like myself?

To prove my theory I will outline another example of how a perfect crime can be perpetrated without the slightest danger of suspicion. Supposing, one day, you notice an old country woman crossing a downtown street, just about to put one foot down on the rails of the streetcar line. The traffic, we will also suppose, is heavy with motorcars, bicycles, and carts. Under these circumstances you would perceive that the old woman is jittery, as is natural for a rustic in a big city. Suppose, now, that at the very moment she puts her foot on the rail a streetcar comes rushing down the tracks toward her. If the old woman does not notice the car and continues across the tracks, nothing will happen. But if someone should happen to shout "Look out, old woman!" what would be her natural reaction? It is superfluous for me to explain that she would suddenly become flustered and would pause to decide whether to go on or to step back. Now, if the motorman of the streetcar could not apply his brakes in time, the mere words "Look out, old woman!" would be as dangerous a weapon as any knife or firearm. I once successfully killed an old country woman in this way— but more of that later.

[Tanaka paused a moment, and a hideous grin contorted his flushed face. Then he continued.]

Yes, in such a case the man who sounds the warning actually becomes a murderer! Who, however, would suspect him of murderous intent? Who could possibly imagine that he had deliberately killed a complete stranger merely to satisfy his lust to kill? Could his action be interpreted in any way other than that of a kindly man bent only on keeping a fellow human being from being run over? There is no ground to suppose even that he would be reproached by the dead! Rather, I should imagine that the old woman would have died with a word of thanks on her lips . . . despite her having been murdered.

Gentlemen, do you now see the beauty of my line of reasoning? Most people seem to believe that whenever a man commits a crime he is sure to be apprehended and swiftly punished. Few, very few, seem to realize that many murderers could go scot-free, if only they would adopt the right tactics. Can you deny this? As can be imagined from the two instances which I have just cited, there are almost limitless ways of committing perfect crimes. For myself, as soon as I discovered the secret I was overjoyed. How generous the Creator was, I told myself blasphemously, to have provided so much opportunity for the perpetration of crimes which can never be detected. Yes, I was quite mad with joy at this discovery. "How wonderful!" I kept repeating. And I knew that once I had put my theories into practice the lives of most people would be completely at the mercy of my whims! Gradually it dawned on me that *murder* offered a key to the problem of relieving my perpetual boredom. Not any ordinary type of murder, I told myself, but murder which would baffle even Sherlock himself! A perfect cure for drowsiness!

During the three years that followed, I gave myself up completely to intensive research in the science of homicide—a pursuit which promptly made me forget my previous boredom. Visualizing myself in the role of a modem Borgia, I swore that I would slay a hundred people before I was done. The only difference, however, would be that instead of using poison I would kill with the weapon of criminal strategy.

Soon I began my career of crime, and just three months ago I marked up a score of ninety-nine lives snuffed out without anyone's knowing that I had been responsible for these deaths. To make the toll an even hundred I had just one more murder to commit. But putting this question aside for a moment, would you like to hear how I killed the first ninety-nine? Of course, I had no grudge against any of them. My only interest was in the art of killing and nothing else. Consequently, I did not adopt the same method twice! Each time my technique differed, for the very effort of thinking up new ways of killing filled my heart with an unholy pleasure.

Actually, however, I cannot take the time to explain each of the ninety-nine ways of murder I used one after another. Therefore I will merely cite four or five of the most outstanding techniques of murder I devised.

A blind masseur who happened to live in my neighborhood became my first victim. As is frequently the case with persons who are incapacitated, he was a very stubborn fellow. For example, if out of kindness someone cautioned him against a certain act, it was his established rule to do exactly the opposite in a manner which plainly said: "Don't make fun of me because I am blind. I can get along without any advice."

One day, while strolling down a busy thoroughfare, I happened to notice the stubborn masseur coming from the opposite direction. Like the conceited fool he was, he was walking fairly swiftly down the road, with his stick on his shoulder, and was humming a song. Not far ahead of him I saw that a deep pit had been dug on the right-hand side of the street by a gang of workers who were repairing the city's sewers. As he was blind and could not see the sign "Danger! Under Repair!" he kept going straight toward the pit, completely free from care. Suddenly a bright idea struck me.

"Hello, Mr. Nemoto," I called in a familiar tone, for I had often had him massage me. The next moment, before he could even return my greeting, I gave my warning. "Look out!" I shouted. "Step aside to the left! Step aside to the left!" This, of course, I called out in a tone of voice which sounded as if I were joking.

Just as I had suspected, the masseur swallowed the bait. Instead of stepping to the left, he kept on walking without altering his course.

"Ha! ha! ha!" he laughed loudly. "You can't fool me!"

Boldly, he took three extra large steps to the right, purposely ignoring my warning, and the next thing he knew, he had stepped right into the pit dug by the sewer workers.

As soon as he fell in I ran up to the edge of the pit, pretending to be very much alarmed and concerned. In my heart, however, I wondered if I had succeeded in killing him. Deep down at the bottom of the hole I saw the man lying crumpled up in a heap, his head bleeding profusely. Looking closer I saw that his nose and mouth were also covered with blood, and his face was a livid, unhealthy yellow. Poor devil! In his fall, he had bitten off his tongue!

A crowd soon gathered, and after much effort we managed to haul him up to the street. When we stretched him out on the pavement he was still breathing, but very faintly. Someone ran off to call an ambulance, but it arrived too late: the poor masseur was no longer of this world.

Thus my plan had worked successfully. And who was there to suspect me? Had I not always been on the best of terms with the man, using his services often? Also, wasn't it *I* who had directed him to step aside to the left in an effort to save him from falling into the pit? With such a perfect setup, even the shrewdest detective could not have suspected even for a fleeting moment that behind my words of "kindly warning" there had lurked a coldly-calculated intention to kill!

Oh, what a terrible way to amuse oneself! And yet, how merry it was! The joy I felt whenever I conceived a new strategy for murder was akin to that of an artist inspired with a new idea for a painting. As for the nervous strain I underwent on each separate occasion, it was doubly compensated for by the overwhelming satisfaction I derived from my successes. Another horrible aspect of my criminal career was that I would invariably look back on the death scenes I had created and, like a vampire smacking his lips after a feast, relish the memory of how the innocent victims of my ruthlessness had spilled their precious life-blood.

Now I shall switch to a new chapter. The season was summer. Accompanied by an old friend of mine, whom I had already selected as my next victim, I went to a remote fishing village in the province of Awa for a vacation. On the beach we found few visitors from the city; most of the swimmers were well-tanned youngsters from the village. Occasionally, along the coast, we saw a few stray students, sketch-books in hand, engrossed in the scenery.

From every viewpoint it was a very lonely, dull place. One big drawback was that there were hardly any of the attractive girls one finds at the more noted bathing resorts. As for our inn, it was like the cheapest of Tokyo boarding houses; the food was unsavory, and nothing, with the sole exception of the fresh raw fish they served, seemed to suit our taste. My friend, however, seemed to be enjoying his stay, never suspecting that I had purposely enticed him here for but one purpose—to murder him.

One day I took him out to a place where the shore suddenly ended in cliffs, quite a distance from the village. Quickly I took off my clothes, shouting: "This is an ideal place for diving!" and stood poised to leap into the water below.

"You're right!" my friend replied. "This is indeed a wonderful place for diving!" And he too began stripping off his clothes.

After standing on the edge of the precipice for a moment, I stretched my arms above my head and shouted in my loudest voice: "One, two, three!" And the next moment I dove headfirst into the water, managing a fairly graceful swan dive. As soon as my head touched the water, however, I twisted my body into an upward curve, so that I actually allowed myself to submerge to a depth of only about four feet. I swam a little at this depth before rising. For me this shallow dive was no marvelous feat, for I had mastered the technique in my early high school days. When I finally popped my head out of the water at a distance of about thirty feet from the shore, I wiped the water off my face and, treading water with my feet, called to my friend.

"Come on in," I shouted. "You can dive as deep as you like. This place is almost bottomless!"

Not suspecting anything, my friend quickly nodded and, poising on the edge of the cliff, dove in. He shot into the water with a splash, but did not reappear for a considerable length of time. This, of course, was no surprise to me, for I knew that there was a large, jagged rock located at a depth of only about eight feet, but quite impossible to detect from atop the cliff. I had probed this sector of the water previously, and everything had suited my plans.

As you may know, the better the diver, the shallower he dives into the water. Being an expert, I had managed to surface without coming into contact with the dangerous rock. But my friend, who was only a novice, had dived into the water to the fullest depth. The result was only natural—death from a crushed skull.

Sure enough, after I had waited for some time, he rose to the surface like a dead tunny, drifting at the mercy of the waves. Playing the role of would-be rescuer, I grabbed him and dragged his floating corpse to the shore. Then, leaving him on the sand, I ran back to the village and sounded the alarm. Promptly some fishermen who happened to be resting after a busy morning of hauling in their nets answered my call for help and accompanied me back to the beach. All along, however, I knew that my friend was beyond all earthly help. Crumpled up on the shore just as I had left him, his head crushed like an eggshell, he was indeed a pitiful sight. Taking just one look, the fishermen all shook their heads.

"There's nothing we can do," they said. "He's already dead!"

In all my life I have been questioned by the police only twice, and this was one of those occasions. As I was the sole witness of the "accident," it was only natural that they should question me. But since the victim and I were known to have been great friends, I was quickly exonerated.

"It is quite obvious," the unsuspecting police said, "that you city folks could not have been aware of the presence of that rock," and the coroner's verdict was "accidental death."

Ironically, I was even offered the condolences of the police officers who had cleared me of all possible guilt. "We are very sorry you have lost your friend" were their very words.

Inwardly, I shrieked with laughter.

Well, as I have said, if I were to recite all my murders one after another, I'm afraid there would be no end. By this time you must surely know what I meant when I spoke of perfect crimes. Every murder that I committed was ingeniously planned beforehand so as to leave no trace of evidence. Once, when I was among the spectators at a circus, I captured the attention of a female tightrope walker who was balancing herself on a high wire by suddenly adopting an extraordinarily strange posture—a posture so strange and obscene that I am ashamed to describe it here. The result, of course, was that she slipped and crashed to her death, because it had been her special pride to walk a tightrope without the benefit of a net. On another occasion, at the scene of a fire, I calmly informed a shrieking woman searching for her child that I had seen him sleeping inside the house. Believing me instantly, she rushed into the flames, while I egged her on with "Can't you hear him crying? He's wailing and wailing for you!" The woman, of course, was burnt to death. And the ironical part of it all was that her child had been safe and sound all along elsewhere.

Another example I could give is the time I saw a girl on the point of trying to decide whether or not to commit suicide by leaping into a river. At the crucial moment, when she had nearly decided to abandon her attempt, I shouted: "Wait!" Caught by surprise, the girl became flustered and, without any further hesitation, dived into the water and was drowned. This, again, was another demonstration of how one seemingly innocent word can end a person's life.

Well, as you may have realized by this time, there is practically no end to my stories. For another thing, the clock on the wall reminds me that the time is getting late. So I'll conclude my narration for this evening with just one more example of how I killed without arousing any suspicion—only this time it is mass murder of which I'll speak.

This case took place last spring. Perhaps you may even remember the report in the newspapers at that time of how a train on the Tokyo-Karuizawa line jumped the tracks and overturned, taking a heavy toll of lives. Well, that's the catastrophe to which I refer.

Actually, this was the simplest trick of all, although it took me a considerable length of time to select a suitable location to carry out my plot. From the very start, however, I had believed I would find it along the line to Karuizawa; this railway ran through lonely mountains, an ideal condition for my plan, and besides, the line had quite a reputation for frequent accidents.

Finally I decided on a precipice near Kumano-Taira Station. As there was a decent spa near the station, I put up at an inn there and pretended to be a long-staying visitor, bathing in the mineral waters daily. After biding my time for about ten days, I felt it would be safe to begin. So one day I took a walk along a mountain path in the area.

After about an hour's walk I arrived at the top of a high cliff a few miles from the inn. Here I waited until the evening shadows fell. Just beneath the cliff the railway tracks formed a sharp curve. On the other side of the tracks yawned a deep ravine, with a swiftly-flowing stream in the mist beyond.

After a while the zero hour I had decided on arrived. Although there was no one there to see, I pretended to stumble and kicked a large rock which had been lying in such a position that this was enough to roll it off the cliff, right down onto the railway tracks. I had planned to repeat the operation over and over again with other rocks if necessary, but I quickly perceived with a thrill that the rock had fallen onto one of the rails, just where I had wanted it.

A down train was scheduled to come along those tracks in half an hour. In the dark, and with the rock lying on the other side of the curve, it would be impossible for the engineer to notice it. After I had thus set the stage for my crime I hurried to Kumano-Taira Station—I knew the walk would take me over half an hour—dashed into the stationmaster's office, and blurted out: "Something terrible has happened!"

All the railway officials looked up anxiously and asked me what I meant.

"I'm a visitor at the spa here," I said, breathing heavily. "I was taking a walk a short while ago along the edge of the cliff above the railway line about four miles from here. Accidentally I stumbled and kicked a rock off the cliff down onto the tracks. Almost immediately I realized that if a train passed there, it would be derailed. So I tried desperately to find a path down to the spot so as to remove the rock, but as I am a stranger in these parts, I could find no way down. Knowing there was not a moment to be lost, I came here as fast as my legs could carry me to warn you. Surely you people can do something to avert a catastrophe."

When I had finished talking the stationmaster paled. "This is a serious matter," he gasped. "The down train just passed this station. By this time it must already have reached that spot!" This, of course, was exactly what I had expected to hear.

Suddenly the phone rang, but even before anyone picked up the receiver, I knew what the report would be. Yes, the worst had happened! The train had jumped the tracks, and two of the coaches had overturned.

Soon I was taken to the village police station for questioning. But my deed had been perpetrated only after long and careful deliberation, so I had all the answers ready. After the interrogation I was released. I had, of course, been severely admonished, but that was all.

So, with just one rock, I had succeeded in taking the lives of no less than seventeen persons in just that one "accident."

Gentlemen, the grand total of the murders I have so far committed numbers ninety-nine. Rather than being penitent, however, I have only become bored with my festival of blood. Today I have but one desire, to make the score an even hundred . . . by taking my own life.

Yes, you may well knit your brows, after hearing of all my cruel acts. Surely not even the devil himself could have surpassed me in villainy. And yet, I still insist that all my wickedness was but the result of unbearable boredom. I killed—but only for the sake of killing! I harbored no malice toward any of my victims. In short, murder was, for me, a sort of game. Do you think I am mad? A homicidal maniac? Of course you do. But I do not care, for I believe I am in good company. Birds of a feather, you know. . . .

On this cynical and insulting note the narrator concluded his disgusting story, his narrow, bloodshot eyes gazing suspiciously into ours.

Suddenly, on the surface of the silk curtains near the door, something began to glitter. At first it looked like a large, silver coin, then like a full moon peering out of the red curtains. Gradually I recognized the mysterious object as a large silver tray held in both hands by a waitress, magically come, as if from nowhere, to serve us drinks. For a fleeting moment I visualized a scene from *Salome,* with the dancing girl carrying the freshly severed head of the prophet on a tray. I even thought that after the tray there would appear from out of the silk curtains a glittering Damascene broadsword, or at least an old Chinese halberd. Gradually my eyes became more accustomed to the wraith-like figure of the waitress, and I gasped with admiration, for she was indeed a beauty! Without any explanation, she moved gracefully among the seven of us and began to serve drinks.

As I took a glass I noticed that my hand was trembling. What strange magic was this, I pondered. Who was she? And where did she come from? Was she from some imaginary world, or was she one of the hostesses from the restaurant downstairs?

Suddenly Tanaka spoke in a casual tone, not at all different from the voice he had used to tell his story—but the words he uttered startled me.

"Now I will shoot you!" were the very words he spoke, having first drawn a revolver from his pocket and aimed it at the girl.

The next instant our cries of surprise, the explosion of the revolver, and the piercing shriek of the girl all seemed to merge. All of us leapt from our seats and lunged at the madman. But then we stopped in our tracks. There, before our eyes, was the woman who had been shot, alive and well, but with a blank look on her face.

"Ha! ha! ha!" Tanaka suddenly burst out laughing in the hysterical tone of a madman. "It's only a toy, only a toy. Ha! ha! You were taken in nicely, Hanako. Ha! ha! . . ."

Was the revolver, then, only a toy, I wondered. From all appearances, it had certainly looked real—with the smoke curling out of the muzzle.

"What a start you gave me!" the waitress cried. She then tried to laugh, but her voice sounded hollow. As for her face, it was as white as a rice cake.

After a moment she went up to Tanaka hesitantly and asked to examine the weapon. Tanaka complied, and the girl looked at the pistol closely.

"Oh, it certainly looks like the real thing, doesn't it?" she exclaimed. "I had no idea it was only a toy." In a playful gesture she suddenly pointed the six-chambered revolver at Tanaka and said: "Now, I'll shoot you and return the compliment."

Bending her left arm, she rested the barrel of the revolver on her elbow and aimed at Tanaka's chest, smiling mischievously.

Instead of showing fright, Tanka only smiled. "Go on, shoot me!" he said teasingly.

"Why not?" the girl retorted, laughing.

Bang! Again the loud explosion seemed to split our eardrums.

This time Tanaka rose from his chair, staggered a couple of steps, and then fell to the floor with a thud. At first we only laughed, although we felt that the joke was becoming stale. But Tanaka continued to remain stretched out on the floor, perfectly still and lifeless, and we again began to feel restless. Was it another of his tricks? It was hard to tell, for it was all uncomfortably realistic. In spite of ourselves, we soon knelt down beside him, although we did not exactly know what to do.

The man who had been sitting next to me took the candelabrum from the table and held it up. By its light we found Tanaka sprawled out grotesquely on the floor, his face contorted. The next moment we got the worst fright of all when we saw his blood oozing out of his chest, dripping onto the floor to form a pool.

From all these indications, we quickly surmised that in the second chamber of the revolver, which he had passed off as only a toy, there had been a real bullet. For a long while we stood there, dumbfounded.

Gradually, I began to reason. Had this all been part of Tanaka's program for the night from the very start? Had he actually been carrying out his threat of ultimately taking his own life to make his score of killings an even hundred? But why did he choose this Red Chamber as the scene for his final deed? Had it been his intention to pin the crime on the waitress? But cer-

tainly she was innocent, for she had not known the pistol was real when she shot him.

Suddenly, I began to see the light. Tanaka's favorite bag of tricks! Yes, that's what it was! Similar to all his other crimes, he had used the waitress to murder him, and yet had made sure that she would not be punished. With six of us as witnesses, she would, of course, be exonerated. Reasoning thus, I knew that I could not be wrong. The "super-killer" had killed for the last time. Each of the other men also seemed to be wrapped in deep meditation. Plainly, I could read their thoughts as being the same as mine.

An eerie silence fell over the company. On the floor the waitress, who had unwittingly become a murderess, was weeping hysterically beside the body of her victim. In all aspects, the tragedy which had occurred in the candlelit Red Chamber seemed altogether too fantastic to be a happening of this world.

All of a sudden a strange voice drowned out the waitress's loud sobs. With an icy chill creeping down my back, I stole a glance at Tanaka, and this time I nearly fainted. Slowly, the "dead man" was staggering to his feet. . . .

In the next tense moment, the "corpse" broke the suspense by bursting into laughter, holding his sides as if to prevent himself from splitting. He then turned to us and said mockingly: "You are indeed a naive audience!"

No sooner had he spoken than another surprise was in store for us. This time the waitress, who had been sobbing on the floor, also got to her feet and began to shake with convulsions of laughter. Rubbing our eyes, we automatically, like robots, returned our gaze to Tanaka.

"What—what happened?" I asked sheepishly. "Are we all bewitched?"

In answer Tanaka said: "Look at this." Still chuckling, he held out a nondescript reddish mass on the palm of his hand and invited us to examine it. "It's a small bag made of the bladder of a cow," he explained. "A few moments ago it contained tomato ketchup and was planted inside my shirt. When the girl fired the blank cartridge, I pressed the bag and pretended to be bleeding. . . . And now, one more confession. The complete life story which I related this evening was nothing but a mass of fabrications from beginning to end. But you must admit I was a pretty good actor. You see, gentlemen, as I had been informed that you were all suffering from boredom, I merely tried to give you some excitement. . . ."

After Tanaka had explained all his tricks, the waitress who had served as his accomplice suddenly pressed the wall-switch. Without warning, a blaze of lights caught all of us huddled in the center of the fantastic room, blinking foolishly at each other. For the first time since joining the group I realized how artificial everything looked in our so-called room of mystery. And as for ourselves, we were just a bunch of fools. . . .

Shortly after Tanaka and the waitress bade us goodnight, we held a special meeting. This time, no stories were told. Instead, we unanimously agreed to disband.

Two Crippled Men

*A*fter emerging from a steaming hot bath the two men settled down to a quiet game of Japanese chess, but after they had completed one long-drawn-out session they shoved aside the chessboard and drifted into conversation. Soft winter sunlight warmed the eight-mat room, lighting up its luxurious paper screens. In the large charcoal brazier, carved out of paulownia wood, before which the two men sat cross-legged on silk cushions, a silver kettle sang cheerfully, the mellow notes drifting out into the landscape garden like a lullaby intended for the baby sparrows dozing on the pine branches.

It was an utterly calm afternoon—monotonous, with nothing happening, but completely restful—and the men's wandering conversation gradually turned to memories of the past. Saito—who was the guest—began by launching into an account of his harrowing experiences in the Battle of Tsingtao during World War I. While his voice droned on and on like the humming of insects, Ihara—the host—listened attentively, from time to time rubbing his hands above the fire in the brazier. During brief lulls in the story the distant song of a

[Certain archaic terms have been amended. Ed.]

nightingale was heard faintly, like musical interludes specially provided to bridge the silences.

When he spoke, Saito's badly disfigured face was horrible to look at; and yet, as he unfolded his thrilling tale of bravery, his grotesque features strangely suited him. He suddenly pointed to a twitch on the right side of his face and explained that it had been caused by splinters from an enemy shell.

"But," he said, "this is not my only reminder of those hectic days. Look! Just look at the rest of my carcass!" With these words, he stripped to the waist and displayed his old scars.

"And to think," he sighed, concluding his tale, "that in my youth I was quite a handsome lad, with a heart overflowing with romantic ambitions. Today, alas, it is all over with me!"

For a few moments Ihara made no comment. Instead, he raised his teacup to his lips two or three times in succession, the deep furrows on his brow indicating that he was lost in thought. The Battle of Tsingtao! Ah, what bloody, tragic times. . . . But he too had been crippled like the other—for the remainder of his life, never more to walk erect, never more to be loved except out of pity! Comparing himself with the other, his friend, Ihara was filled with envy. For one thing, the other had won his scars with honor! As for himself . . . the very thought of his own history sent cold shivers running up and down his spine. Suddenly he looked up and met Saito's eyes gazing intently into his own.

"Well, Ihara," Saito remarked, "now it's your turn. I don't believe you've ever told me the story of your past."

Ihara moistened his lips with green tea; then he cleared his throat.

"I would hardly call it a story," he began. "Rather, it is more of a confession. However, compared to your exploits, I fear my words will prove exceedingly dull."

"Nevertheless, I insist on hearing them," Saito said, his eyes lighting up with keen interest.

Ihara caught the gleam in the other's eyes, and for a split second he was startled. He fancied that somewhere, at some time in the past, he had caught that same look, that same flicker of the eyelashes. They had met only ten days ago. Could it have been since then, or wasn't it much, much further in the past?

Ihara was truly mystified. Somewhere in the back of his mind, he suspected some supernatural reason for his having met the other at this inn ten days ago, for their having immediately struck up so close a friendship. He just couldn't seem to convince himself that their chance meeting was merely a coincidence . . . that two crippled birds should just happen to come together. There was, however, one thing of which he was absolutely certain: he had met the other somewhere before. But exactly where . . . and under what circumstances? This nagging feeling of vague recognition puzzled him. Possibly they had played together as children . . . or possibly . . .

"I'm still waiting to hear your story," Saito suddenly broke in.

"I was merely trying to arrange all the data in my mind before beginning. You must remember that this is the first time I've ever attempted to tell my story to any living soul." Thus Ihara began his strange narrative, while the other leaned forward in the attitude of one anxious not to miss even a single word.

I was born [Ihara recalled] the eldest son of a shopkeeper in the town of Onuki. From the very start my parents indulged me too much, and I think this is why I acquired such a weak character in my childhood. In primary school my failings were quickly recognized, and before long I found myself two classes behind my original classmates. Gradually, however, I seemed to recover from my lethargy.

Thus the years sped by, and I eventually came to Tokyo to enter Waseda University. Blessed with fairly good health, and eager to succeed in my studies, I found life in the big city far more pleasant than I had originally anticipated. True, I experienced many inconveniences living in cheap lodgings, but taking all daily vicissitudes gaily, I enjoyed rather than brooded over my lot as a struggling student.

Looking back on those early days, I realize now that they were actually the best years of my life. At any rate, I had hardly been in Tokyo for a full year when a most disturbing incident look place.

[At this point Ihara shivered slightly, but it was not from cold. Saito dropped a half-smoked cigarette into the brazier, his eyes not once leaving the face of the narrator.]

One morning [Ihara continued] I was getting ready to go to school when a friend who lived in the same lodging house entered my room. To my surprise, he slapped me on the shoulder and complimented me on my "eloquent oration of the night before."

Deeply puzzled by his words, I said: "What do you mean by my 'eloquent oration?' I don't know what you're talking about!"

My friend put his hands on his hips and roared with boisterous laughter. "Come now, don't be so modest," he shot back. "Don't you remember last night? You burst into my room long after I had gone to bed, woke me up roughly, and engaged me in a complicated argument. Surely you remember. I don't think you were drunk."

"Surely you must be mistaken," I quickly replied. "As far as I know, I didn't even go near your room last night, much less engage you in any debate."

"Oh, stop pulling my leg," the other answered. "You know perfectly well that you came to my room last night to argue, even quoting freely from the philosophies of Plato and Aristotle. In any event, I didn't come here to complain of your conduct, but to tell you that your argument impressed me deeply. In fact, after you left, some of the statements you made lingered so long in my mind that I couldn't go back to sleep. As a result, I sat up reading and then wrote this postcard." My fellow lodger waved a written postcard in my face, asking if he could possibly have written it unless someone had awakened him after he had gone to sleep.

I agreed that he couldn't, but after he left I felt confused and unhappy. This was indeed a disturbing turn of events if ever there was one, for as sure as I sit here now, sane and human, I had not the slightest recollection of having made any oration the night before. A few minutes later I went to the university, still deeply perplexed.

In the lecture hall, we were waiting for the professor to arrive, when somebody suddenly tapped me on the shoulder. Wheeling around, I saw my fellow lodger.

"Do you happen to have the habit of talking in your sleep?" he asked casually. This remark of his startled me, because during my grade school days I had indeed had such a habit.

"I—I did once," I quickly replied, "but not any more. People have told me that I sometimes acted strangely as a child, often seeming to be in a trance. And my parents say I used to talk in my sleep, and that when someone playfully engaged me in conversation while I was deep in slumber, I would reply— clearly and sensibly—but would not remember anything the following morning. No one, however, seemed worried about this; even the doctor who was consulted stated definitely that it was not a cause for any alarm. 'Just a slight case of sleep-talking, a slight touch of somnambulism' was his diagnosis. Naturally, I was much talked about in the neighborhood, because sleepwalking is a little unusual, but gradually, as I grew up, these nocturnal conversations grew less frequent, until finally it seemed that I was cured."

After listening to my story, my companion observed that possibly I had started again. "Now that you mention somnambulism," he said, "I do recall that you seemed a little odd last night. For example, your face was a complete blank, and your eyes were staring. The pupils of your eyes were dilated, but when I brought the lamp close to you they contracted quickly. Also, sometimes, your eyes were partly or entirely shut, flickering open only briefly as if you were registering your surroundings in your mind with photographic clarity."

When I heard these words I began to feel even more uneasy. I didn't quite know what to make of the term "somnambulism"—nor exactly what tragic implications it held. From what I had heard about sleepwalking in the past, I understood that it was a state in which the body came under the control of the subconscious. As I began to think about what this might mean to me, I began to shudder. Supposing, I told myself, I were to commit some crime during one of my trances?

Two days later I was a complete mental wreck. Unable to eat, and naturally unable to sleep for fear I would commit some violence while in the mysterious realm of the subconscious, I realized that I would never have another moment of peace unless I had medical help. So I went to see a doctor I knew.

After examining me, the doctor told me frankly that I was a somnambulist. "But you need have no undue fears," he added, with what I considered unwarranted optimism. "Actually, yours is not a very serious case—provided you do not aggravate your condition by overstraining your mental energies. Calm yourself as much as you can; try to live a regular, normal, healthy life; and I am sure you will be cured."

With these words he dismissed me, but I was far from relieved. Quite to the contrary, now that I definitely *knew* myself to be a somnambulist, I began to worry even more. Losing complete interest in my studies, I wasted away the hours of each day doing nothing but fretting over my fate—often wishing that I had never been born.

The days dragged on, every daylight hour like a century of agony; yet they were nothing compared to the tortures that awaited me at night. Fearing the unknown, I dared not sleep except in snatches. At last, however, a whole month had passed without a single untoward incident, and I began to feel somewhat reassured. "Maybe the doctor was right after all," I told myself. "If I can just stop worrying, I'll be fine."

I was on the point of believing that I had been making a mountain out of a molehill, and that if anything, I was just a victim of badly shattered nerves—when something dreadful happened, again casting me into the deepest abyss of despair.

One morning, shortly after getting up, I found an unfamiliar object—somebody's watch—ticking loudly a few inches away from my pillow. With all my previous fears again surging into my breast like mad ocean waves, I picked the watch up with a shaking hand and tried to figure out to whom it could possibly belong. Suddenly, as if in answer to my fears, I heard a shout from an adjoining room.

"I can't find my watch! I can't find my watch!" someone yelled, and I immediately recognized the voice as that of another lodger in the same house, a clerk employed by a trading company.

"So it's happened at last!" I told myself. "Just as I feared, I've committed a crime—without knowing it." Perspiring profusely and my heart beating wildly, I rushed to the room of my schoolmate and asked for his assistance in returning the watch, which I had evidently stolen from the clerk. My friend agreed and took the watch back to the clerk. Once he had explained that I was a somnambulist, the clerk was very understanding and agreed to consider the incident closed and forgotten.

After that shocking incident, however, word quickly got around that I was an incurable sleepwalker. Even in my classroom, I knew that the other students were talking about me behind my back.

With all my heart I yearned to be cured of my horrible affliction. There had to be a way out—some way out—and I was determined to find it, regardless of whatever sacrifice this might entail. Every day I bought and read books by the armful, tried various types of calisthenics to improve my health, and consulted several doctors. Far from improving, however, my condition went from bad to worse.

At first, the fits came over me only once or twice a month, fits in which my subconscious mind completely dominated my actions. And every time I learned what had happened only by seeing what I had taken or what I had left behind in some unfamiliar place. If only I hadn't left these evidences of my nocturnal wanderings, I told myself, it wouldn't be so bad. And yet, if I did not leave any evidence, then how was I ever to know what type of felony I had unconsciously committed?

One night I strayed out of my lodging house at about midnight and began to wander about the graveyard of a temple in the neighborhood. It happened that one of the office clerks who lived in the same house with me was returning from a late party, and as he came along the street beside the graveyard, he caught sight of my quietly moving figure beyond the low hedge. He quickly spread the report that a ghost was haunting the temple grounds. Later, when it was discovered that *I* had been the "ghost," I became the laughingstock of the whole neighborhood.

But, as you can well imagine, it was no laughing matter for me. Instead, it was a horrible tragedy from which I now seemed to have no escape. As for the nights—those quiet moments of darkness and calm which spell restfulness to all ordinary human beings—they meant but one thing so far as I was concerned—*fear*. My state of mind finally became such that I grew to fear the very word "night"—and everything connected with the ritual of sleep.

Meanwhile, I continued to delve deeper and deeper into the workings of the human mind. What strange mechanism makes one act so abnormally, I asked myself over and over again. I was thankful that, despite all my anguish, I had not so far committed a serious crime. But what would happen, I asked myself, if I were to become responsible for some fatal tragedy? According to the many books on sleepwalking which I had accumulated and read with deepest absorption, ghastly crimes had been committed by somnambulists. Was it then not possible that I too might commit some such bloody act as murder?

Once caught in this web of thought, I could contain myself no longer. Deciding that the best course was to abandon my studies and return home, I wrote a long letter to my parents, explaining all the circumstances and asking their advice. And it was while I waited impatiently for a reply that the very catastrophe which I most feared actually came to pass. . . .

All this while Saito had been sitting motionless on his square cushion, taking in every word as if hypnotized. Outside, the sun was beginning to set, and as the New Year bustle of this popular hot-spring resort was now over, the absolute stillness seemed ominous.

During the brief pause which he allowed himself, Ihara eyed Saito intently, trying to fathom the other's reaction to his story, while simultaneously trying to place the strange resemblance of his listener to another face which he had once known . . . somewhere. . . . Still unable to remember where, he again picked up the thread of his narrative:

To return to my story, the most shocking moment of my life came in the fall of 1907. . . a long time ago, to be sure. However, I remember every detail as if it had all taken place yesterday.

One morning I was suddenly awakened from a restless sleep by a loud noise in the house. Quickly I got out of bed, deeply alarmed. "Did I have another fit during the night?" was the first question I asked myself. If so, what had I done? Secretly praying that it was nothing serious, I glanced quickly around the room, and suddenly I saw a mysterious bundle, in a cloth wrapper, placed just inside the door of my room.

Under normal circumstances I would have examined the contents of the unknown parcel, but in this particular case I was too gripped with fear and foreboding to act rationally. So instead of even attempting to satisfy my curiosity, I snatched up the bundle and threw it into the closet. This done, I looked around furtively, like a thief, and only after I had made absolutely certain that I had been unobserved did I emit a sigh of relief. Just then someone knocked on my door, and when I opened it I found a fellow lodger standing outside in the narrow corridor, his face pale as a sheet.

"Say, Ihara," the man said with a shiver, "something terrible's happened! Old man Murata, our landlord, has been murdered. Everybody suspects a burglar, but you'd better come along and join the rest of us. Someone has already telephoned the police, and they'll soon be here!"

You can well imagine how I felt when I heard this tragic news. My heart stopped beating, my tongue was glued to the roof of my mouth, and I could not utter a sound. As in a nightmare, I followed the other to the scene of the tragedy.

The ghastly sight which met my eyes there made me all but faint. Even now, twenty long years later, I can still see the eyes of the dead old keeper of the lodging house staring madly and boring right into my own—as if in silent accusation.

[Ihara paused again and with the sleeve of his kimono wiped away the beads of perspiration that dotted his brow.]

Yes [he continued with a shudder], I can remember every detail vividly. From the excited chatter of the others in the room, I managed to learn the details of what had evidently taken place. It seemed that on the particular night of the tragedy the old housekeeper had slept alone in his room. The next morning one of the maids had thought it strange that he was not yet awake since he had always been the first to rise, and she had gone to awaken him and made her gruesome discovery. When he was found, old man Murata was lying flat on his back, strangled in his sleep with the flannel muffler he had always worn, even to bed.

Soon the police arrived on the scene. In looking for evidence, they discovered that several items belonging to the dead man were missing, namely, the keys which he had always kept in his purse, plus a large fortune in securities which had disappeared together with the small portable cash-box in which they had been kept. Also, further examination showed that the main door had not been locked on the preceding night because he had expected his wife and son to return late. So it had been quite a simple matter for the murder or murderers to gain admission to the house. As for on-the-spot clues, there was but one item—a soiled handkerchief—and this the police officers took with them for minute laboratory inspection.

Meanwhile, after I had seen enough of the murder scene to want to linger any longer, I stealthily withdrew to my own room. After I had locked the door, my first thought flew to the closet where I had hidden the mysterious bundle. "What's in it?" I asked myself with horror. "Is this to be a real case of a skeleton in a closet?" Even before I took out the bundle and examined the contents, I knew what I would find. Inside the package, I found the victim's missing securities.

Not long after, the police took me into custody. Even without the damaging evidence of the stolen securities, which the police found in my possession, the case against me seemed conclusive, for the handkerchief which had been found at the scene of the crime was mine.

The days that followed were like a nightmare. Cast into a cell, I was questioned incessantly for hours on end. Finally, they brought along a mental specialist—a psychiatrist I believe he was—and after asking his expert opinion as to my case, the police also called various tenants of the lodging house to give testimony. Many who knew me well testified that, so far as they knew, I came from a respectable family and that they could not imagine me turning into a ruthless killer just for the sake of money. Others swore that I was a sleepwalker, and promptly cited several instances where, they claimed, I had acted abnormally, but without seeming to be conscious of my own conduct.

Another person who testified was my father, who came up specially from our home town to try to save me from hanging. I remember that he hired three lawyers for my defense.

Other witnesses for the defense were my friend Kimura—the very person who first discovered that I was a somnambulist—and several of my classmates. Even now, my heart goes out in gratitude to these staunch friends, for they spared no effort on my behalf.

As was to be expected in so complicated an affair, the trial which eventually got under way dragged on and on, with the prosecution and defense waging a bitter struggle. Fortunately for me, however, the testimony of the many witnesses for the defense was so convincing that I was finally handed the verdict of *not guilty.*

But, you are sorely mistaken if you think even for a moment that this verdict restored my peace of mind. Now, although I was declared innocent, the murder still remained to be solved. Who had done it? Inside my tortured mind a terrifying voice kept repeating: "You are a murderer! You are a fiend! You have cheated the rope, but you cannot escape your own conscience!"

As soon as I was free, I went home with my father, and shortly afterward, I fell desperately ill. Had it been a physical ailment, I would no doubt have soon recovered. But this was something different—a mystic mental disease for which there seemed to be no known cure. Finally, after six months, I managed to get up, but all the time I knew, and so did my family, that I was no longer normal. Instead I was a man without a soul—a mental cripple destined to live the remainder of my life in anguish and misery. Thus did my normal life end.

Soon after, my younger brother succeeded my father as head of the family, while I continued to live on as a parasite, always dependent upon the labor, compassion, and resources of others. In this way, twenty miserable years have dragged by—and today I am the monstrosity that you see before you—seemingly normal outside, but a hideous cripple inside. Compared to the ugliness of my mental structure, Mr. Saito, I consider your physical features to be positively handsome.

The narrator's face broke into a smile, and he repeated: "Yes, you're handsome, my good man. Compared to me, you're handsome!" Caught by the ironic humor of his own statement, Ihara broke into an eerie laugh. After a while, however, he quieted down and drew the tea things nearer to him. "Forgive me," he apologized, noticing the other's frowning. "I was not laughing at you—no one but myself can appreciate the humor of my life story."

Saito cleared his throat. "A tragic story indeed," he commented. "Strange how wrong one can be in one's first impressions. From the very first time I saw you, I took you to be a contented man of leisure. But tell me one thing. Are you still a somnambulist? Do you still wander in your sleep and . . . er . . . commit crimes?"

Ihara smiled again. "Strange to relate," he replied, "I have never had another fit since the old man was murdered. According to the opinion of different doctors, my 'somnambulistic nerves' must have been paralyzed by the shock I suffered at the lodging house. Can you now imagine why I laughed at myself a moment ago? Can't you realize what a comic figure I have cut these past twenty years, wasted in fear of something which was never more to happen?"

Again, Ihara began to laugh, but Saito cut him short. "One moment," he said. "Tell me something about that friend of yours at the lodging house—the man you called Kimura. He

was the one who first called attention to your somnambulism, wasn't he?"

Ihara nodded. "Yes, he was the first to find out," he replied. "But then, there were also the others—the man who swore that his watch had been stolen, and later the man who spread the alarm that I had been prowling around like a ghost in the cemetery."

"But were these the only occasions which made you think that you were a sleepwalker?" Saito asked, his eyes gleaming through narrow slits. "Weren't there any other incidents?"

"Yes, many," Ihara replied. "Once, another lodger said that he heard footsteps late one night along the corridor of the house, while another accused me of trying to break into his room. . . But why all these questions? What are you driving at?"

Saito forced a laugh. "Forgive me," he said softly. "I wasn't trying to cross-examine you. I just couldn't convince myself that a man of your high intelligence would be capable of doing such things without being aware of what he was doing. You, of course, call it somnambulism. But I am not quite satisfied. You know it is quite common for people who are deformed, and live aloof from the world, like me, to be very skeptical, so I find all this hard to believe. How can sleepwalkers know what they're doing? They can only believe what they are told by others. Even a doctor knows only what he's told about a case like this. Unless they are told what you are supposed to have done, it is absolutely impossible for them to diagnose a case as somnambulism. Now, maybe I'm just a suspicious fool, a born skeptic apt even to disbelieve that the world is round; but I want to ask you: Are you certain—positively, absolutely certain— that you really *did* walk in your sleep? If you aren't, don't you think that you were a little too gullible and naive in immediately swallowing what others told you?"

Hearing these words, Ihara began to fidget, while in the pit of his stomach he suddenly felt a sickening sensation. Actually, it was not because of what the other had said—but the way in which he had said it. Staring back at the other's grim countenance, Ihara again seemed to sense that he had seen this ugly mask somewhere before. However, he replied: "I didn't really believe it at first. But gradually, when these fits became more frequent—"

Saito again interrupted. "Please don't argue without facts," he said sternly. "How—*how* did you know that your fits became more frequent?"

"Because I was told—" Ihara stopped short. Yes, the other was right. He had only had the word of others about what he had done.

Saito immediately took advantage of the other's hesitation. "There—you see?" he gloated. "At no time were you sure! On every occasion it was the word of someone else—of that so-called friend Kimura, for example!"

"Yes, but there were others," Ihara broke in. "There was the clerk who discovered me at the cemetery, the man who missed his watch, the man who saw me break into his room. . . . Besides, what about the many clues I left behind me? Don't forget, every time I had a fit, I left something behind, or took something away. Certainly, things can't move by themselves!"

"That's the most suspicious point of all," insisted Saito. "Even a fool knows that things could easily be moved or planted here and there if there's something to be gained by doing so. And as for your many witnesses, I don't consider any of them to be trustworthy. Take, for example, the man who found you prowling in the graveyard. After constantly hearing that you were a somnambulist, wouldn't he have identified you as the 'ghost' whether you were or not? The same goes for all the others. I tell you, man, that from everything you have told me I am strongly inclined to believe that you were the victim of a clever hoax by someone who was using you for his own purposes. I'll even tell you who that culprit was! He was none other than *Kimura,* the man who had always posed as your friend!"

"Kimura?" Ihara gasped.

"None other," the other emphasized strongly. "Now look here. Let's say that Kimura harbors a strong grudge against the landlord and wants to kill him. Like all criminals, however, he's afraid of getting caught. What, then, is his first logical move? To seek a scapegoat, of course, some poor innocent fool who will bear all the suspicion. Now, under these circumstances, would it not have been convenient for him to choose you—a credulous and weak-minded man—for that very role? Once he was decided, the rest was easy. After getting your admission that you had once suffered from somnambulism in your child-hood, he carefully and skilfully wove his plot. First, he aroused your apprehension about your mental condition. Next, he stole small objects, such as the watch you mentioned, and planted them in your room while you were asleep. Another detail was to disguise himself like you and to wander about in the ceme-tery. Finally, after the plot was well-prepared, and with your 'sleepwalking' well-established, he murdered the old man, planted one of your handkerchiefs at the scene of the crime, and likewise planted the old man's securities in your room. . . . There's the whole story from a different angle—an angle which you no doubt never considered, but which is neverthe-less quite possible!"

When Ihara heard this amazing theory, his whole frame be-gan to tremble. "But—but what about Kimura's conscience?" he blurted out. "Supposing I had been convicted of the murder and sentenced to the gallows? Would he have allowed an in-nocent man to be executed for his own crime?"

Saito gave a weird chuckle. "There," he said, "you have a point, but my theory covers that as well. Do you imagine, even for a moment, that a somnambulist would be convicted of a crime which he did not know he had committed? In the Middle Ages it may have been possible, but not today. No, my friend, Kimura knew all along that you would be acquitted, and so he didn't worry about you!"

After thus finishing expounding his theory, Saito paused briefly and eyed his companion intently. Then he went on in a new tone of voice.

"Forgive me, Mr. Ihara, for having suggested all these possibilities," he said. "I only mentioned them because I was greatly moved by your confession. If you still believe that you really did kill a man while in a trance, there is nothing further I can say or do to change your mind. However, I hope that the theory I've outlined will help lessen your mental anguish hereafter."

Ihara heard the consoling words, but his thoughts were elsewhere. "Why?" he muttered aloud. "Why did Kimura murder the old man? What reason could he possibly have had? Was it revenge? Only *he* can explain this!" Slowly he raised his eyes and stared into his companion's eyes. Saito, however, looked down at the floor. Softly, winter shadows had begun playing over the foliage in the garden, and all at once the crippled ex-soldier suddenly shivered with cold.

"It's become chilly again," he remarked, rising nervously. "I'm off to take another bath."

Still avoiding the other's piercing look, he quietly sneaked out of the room like some skulking animal.

Left to himself, Ihara continued to stare, eyes bloodshot with fury, at the doorway through which the other had departed, clutching in his hand the steel chopsticks from the brazier and jabbing them into the ashes. After a long moment the hardened look on his face relaxed and was finally replaced by a bitter smile playing around his mouth.

"The devil!" he cursed. "I should have known he was Kimura all along!"

The
Traveler with the
Pasted Rag Picture

If this story I am about to tell was not a dream or a series of hallucinations, then that traveler with the pasted rag picture must have been mad. Or it may even be that I actually did catch a glimpse of one corner of another world as if through a magic crystal, just as a dream often carries one into the realms of the supernatural, or as a madman sees and hears things which we, the normal, are quite incapable of perceiving.

One warm, cloudy day in the dim past, I was on my way home from a sight-seeing trip to Uotsu, the town on the Japan Sea noted for its many mirages. Whenever I tell this story, those who know me well often contradict me, pointing out that I have never been to Uotsu. Then I find myself in a greater quandary than ever, for I do not have even a shred of evidence to prove that I have actually been there, and I begin to ask myself: "Was it only a dream after all?"

But, if so, how account for the vivid colors I distinguished in the "dream?" It is well known, as all dreamers will agree, that scenes which appear on the screen of the subconscious mind are quite devoid of color, like the flickerings of a black-and-white motion picture. But even now that scene of the interior of the railway carriage flashes back vividly to my mind,

[Certain British spellings and archaic terms have been amended. Ed.]

especially the garish rag picture with its striking colors of purple and crimson, with the dark, piercing, snake-like eyes of the two figures depicted there.

It had only been a short time previously that I had seen a mirage for the first time in my life. Originally I had expected a mirage to be something like an ancient painting—perhaps a beautiful palace floating serenely on a sea of mist—but at the sight of a real mirage, I was startled, to say the least. There, at Uotsu, under the gnarled branches of old pine trees lining the silvery beach, I and a large group of other visitors gazed expectantly at the expansive sky and sea. Never had any sea seemed so unnaturally devoid of sound. It was an eerie and ominous gray, without even a ripple, looking more like an endless swamp.

Gazing as far as my eyes could reach, I noticed that there was no line marking the horizon, for sea and sky were merged into a thick, grayish haze. And above this haze, a large, ghost-like, white sail suddenly loomed, gliding along smoothly and serenely.

As for the mirage itself, it seemed as though a few drops of India ink had been spilt on the surface of a milk-colored film and then projected enormously against the sky. The forests of the distant Noto Peninsula were vaguely and enormously magnified, like black worms placed under a microscope and seen through a badly focused lens. At times it also took on the aspect of a strangely shaped cloud. But the location of a real cloud is clearly distinguishable, whereas in this case I discovered that the distance between the mirage and its observer was oddly unmeasurable. This uncertainty of distance made the mirage even more eerie than I had ever imagined it would be.

Sometimes the mirage took the form of a horrible ogre floating in the distant sky; then, swiftly, it would assume another hazy and monstrous shape looming inches away from my face. At other times, it was like a huge, blackish dot seen directly before my eyes. A moment later, a mammoth-sized, quivering triangle would begin to grow bit by bit; then, suddenly, it too would collapse without warning. Quickly, the same indescribable mass would appear again, this time stretching horizontally and running like a long train. But again the shape would scatter before it could be brought properly into focus, transforming itself into something resembling a row of fir trees.

And yet, despite all these changes of form, each transitional process was so subtle and gradual as to be imperceptible. Perhaps the magical power of this mirage had bewitched us all. If so, then it may well have been that the same uncanny power continued to hold me in its grasp even on the train carrying me homeward. After standing and staring at the mysterious scenes projected on the sky for two hours on end, I must say that I was in a most peculiar frame of mind as I left Uotsu for the night's journey home.

It was exactly six o'clock in the evening when I boarded the Tokyo-bound train at Uotsu Station. For some strange reason—or was it a usual thing with the trains on that line?—the second-class carriage which I occupied was almost as empty as a church after services. As I stepped into the car I found only one solitary passenger snuggled comfortably in the farthest corner.

Soon the train got underway, the locomotive chugging away monotonously as it pulled its heavy load along the deserted seacoast, then groaning and wheezing as it began to climb. Deep in the mist of the marsh-like sea, the crimson evening glow was now barely discernible. A white sail which looked weirdly large glided smoothly in the haze. It was a sultry evening, the air seemingly bereft of all oxygen—even the occasional breezes which stole into the car through the open window were weak and thin. A series of short tunnels and rows of wooden posts erected as snow-breaks flickered past, making the scenery of the sea and sky play a game of hide-and-seek in my vision.

As the train rumbled past the precipice of Oyashirazu, dusk closed in upon us. Just at this moment, the other passenger in the dimly lit coach stirred in his corner and stood up. Watching him without any particular reason, I saw him spread a large wrapping cloth of black satin on his seat. In it he began to wrap a flat object about two feet by three in size which had hitherto been propped up against the window. Somehow the man's movements gave me a creepy feeling.

The flat object, which I supposed must be some kind of tablet, had until then been resting with its front side turned to the windowpane, and I began to wonder why. Now, as he moved the object, I caught a glimpse of the front side and saw it was a garish rag picture, strangely vivid and different from usual examples of this minor art.

My curiosity aroused, I looked closely at the owner of this strange object and was startled to note that he himself was even stranger in appearance. Thin and long-legged, he wore an old fashioned sack coat tailored with narrow lapels and drooping shoulders and trousers of an equally outmoded and narrow cut. At first glance he made a rather comical figure. But as I continued to gaze I began to realize that his outdated attire was oddly becoming to him.

His face was pale and thin, with features which clearly distinguished him as a man of above normal intelligence. But what impressed me most were his eyes, which seemed to gleam with an uncanny light. Looking at his black and glossy hair neatly parted in the middle, I guessed him to be about forty years old. But I quickly added another twenty years when I noticed his face networked with numerous wrinkles. In fact, it may have been the complete disparity between his black, glossy hair and his multi-wrinkled face which caused me to feel so uneasy.

After he had finished wrapping up his tablet, he suddenly looked up in my direction. Caught by surprise, I had no time to turn away, and our eyes met. Seeing him smile, shyly, I returned his greeting with a nod.

While the train rumbled past two more stations, we kept to our own seats at opposite ends of the carriage, occasionally stealing a glance at each other, and then looking away quickly with embarrassment when caught in the act.

Outside, it was now quite dark. Pressing my face against the window glass, I looked out and could see nothing but the solitary lamp of a fishing boat twinkling far out at sea. Through the boundless darkness, it seemed as if our long, gloomy carriage were the only existing world, monotonously rumbling along on its creaky wheels, my peculiar companion and I the only creatures alive. Not a single new passenger had boarded our second-class coach, and, strange to recall, not even the conductor or train boy had put in an appearance.

As I watched the stranger in the far corner, my mind began to play strange tricks. For one fleeting moment he appeared to be some unholy foreign magician, and gradually a terrible fear began to gnaw at my heart. When there is no distraction to alleviate it, fear is an emotion which steadily grows in intensity. When I finally felt that I could stand the suspense no longer, I got to my feet and walked down the aisle toward the stranger. The very fear I had of him seemed to drag me toward him.

Reaching his seat, I sat down on the facing seat and, with narrowed eyes, peered closely at his furrowed face. My breathing was constricted practically to the point of suffocation.

All along I had been keenly aware that the man had been gazing at me from the moment I had risen from my seat. And then suddenly, before I had even recovered my breath, he spoke in a dry voice.

"Is this what you want to see?" he asked, nodding his head casually toward the flat parcel beside him.

I was so taken aback by the suddenness of his question that I found myself completely tongue-tied. The tone of his voice had been natural enough—so completely natural, in fact, that it further disarmed me.

"I'm sure you're dying of curiosity to see this," he said again, calling me back to my senses with a jolt.

"Yes—yes, if you would permit me," I stammered, feeling my face flushing.

"It would be a great pleasure," the old man replied with a disarming smile. Then he added: "I've been expecting you to ask me for some time."

He unwrapped the large cloth covering carefully with his long fingers and stood the tablet against the window again, this time facing me.

Unconsciously, I closed my eyes, although why, I could never explain. I simply felt that I had to. But finally, with a supreme effort, I forced my eyes open, and for the first time I saw—the thing!

It was just an ordinary wooden tablet, with a picturesque scene painted on its surface. The scene showed a suite of rooms, their floors covered with mats of pale-green straw, and their ceilings, painted in assorted colors, seemed to stretch far away into the distance, like the backdrops of the Kabuki theater. In the left foreground there was a classical window, painted with bold brush strokes, while beneath it there reposed a low, black writing desk, which seemed utterly out of place.

Against this background, there were two figures, each about one foot high, looming in bold relief, having been fashioned out of cloth and pasted on the tablet. One was a white-haired old man, garbed in a well-worn, black velvet suit of an obsolete European cut, sitting stiffly on the floor. And, strangely enough, this figure bore a striking resemblance to the old man sitting beside me. Shifting my gaze, I examined the other figure, which was that of a strikingly beautiful girl no older than seventeen or so. Her coiffure was of the classical style, while her

intricately designed kimono was a long-sleeved affair of crimson artistically blended with other lighter hues, held together with a gorgeous black satin sash. Her posture was delicately amorous, for she was leaning shyly against the lap of the old man, as in a typical Japanese love scene on the stage.

In sharp contrast to the crudeness of the setting, the elaborateness of the pasted rag dolls was astonishing. The faces were fashioned out of white silk, with uncannily realistic wrinkles. As for the girl's hair, it was real, affixed strand by strand, and dressed with intricate skill. The old man's white hair too was no less real. As for his clothes, I noticed that even the seams were faithfully sewn. The buttons too, small as millet seeds, were there.

To add to all this, I also saw the swelling of the girl's breasts, the bewitching line about her thighs, the scarlet crepe of her undergarments showing from beneath her kimono, the natural fleshy texture of her white skin, the shell-like nails on her fingers. . . . In fact, all was so perfect and true to life that I even thought I could have found pores and downy hair if I had continued my scrutiny through a magnifying glass.

The tablet itself appeared very old; the colors of the background had peeled off here and there, and the costumes of the pair were faded in color. Despite these flaws, however, the two figures were so uncannily real that one would have expected them to come to life at any moment.

In the classical puppet theater I have often experienced the sensation of seeing a doll, manipulated by a real master of the art, momentarily come to life. But the two rag figures pasted on the tablet had not just a fleeting aliveness, but a permanent one.

Lost in my wonder, I had almost forgotten the old man beside me. But suddenly he gave a cackle of delight.

"Do you realize the truth now, my good man?"

After uttering this cryptic remark, he took the black leather case which had been hanging by a strap over one shoulder and calmly began to unlock it with a small key. Then, taking out a very old pair of binoculars, he held them out to me.

"Look through these," he invited.

I was reaching for the glasses when he interrupted: "No, no, you're standing too near. Step back a little. . . . There, that's better."

Although it was a strange invitation, I was gripped by an intense curiosity. The binoculars were strangely shaped, and their leather case was worn with age and use, its inner layer of brass showing here and there. Like the clothes of their owner, the binoculars too were quite a museum piece.

Taking the proffered binoculars, I raised them casually to my eyes. But the old man suddenly cried out so piercingly that I almost dropped the glasses.

"No, no, no! Wait, wait! You're holding them the wrong way!" he shrieked wildly. "Don't—don't ever do that again!"

Startled by the outcry and the insane light gleaming in his eyes, I lowered the instrument and mumbled a hasty apology, although for the life of me I could not understand the reason for his sudden consternation.

Raising the binoculars again, this time in the proper way, I began to adjust the lenses, and gradually there came into focus an amazingly large image of the girl on the tablet—her white skin glistening with an utterly natural luster, and her entire body seeming to move.

Within the confines of the antique nineteenth-century binoculars which I held in my trembling hands, there vividly existed another world, entirely alien from my own. And, within this realm, there lived and breathed the gorgeous young girl, incongruously enjoying a tête-à-tête with the white-haired old man who was surely old enough to be her grandfather.

"This must be witchcraft!" I unconsciously warned myself. But like a person caught in a hypnotic trance, I found it impossible to avert my eyes.

Although I could see that the girl was quite immobile, her whole appearance seemed to have undergone a complete transformation. She now seemed to be a totally different creature from the one I had scrutinized with my naked eye. But whatever the changes which had been wrought, they were all to the good. Now her whole body seemed to quiver with life. Her pale face had turned a rosy pink. And as for her breasts— they now seemed to be actually pulsing beneath her thin, silken kimono.

After I had feasted my delighted eyes on every inch of her luscious, delicately-molded body, I turned the glasses on the happy, white-haired old man against whom the girl was leaning. He too seemed to live and breathe in the realm of the binoculars. As I watched, speechless with wonder, it seemed that he was trying to embrace this girl who was but a mere child compared to his venerable old age. But quickly I also caught another expression on his wrinkled face—a terrifying mixture of grief and agony.

At this point I began to imagine that I was caught up in the terrors of a nightmare, and, by sheer force of will, I pulled the binoculars down and looked around. But nothing had changed. There I was, still standing in the dimly lit railway coach, with the pasted rag picture on the tablet and the old man, plus the darkness outside, filling my gaze, with the same monotonous rumbling of the train's wheels vibrating in my ears.

"You look deadly pale," my strange companion remarked, eyeing me intently.

"Can I help it. . . after what I've seen?" I replied nervously. "For a moment I thought I'd gone insane."

He ignored my words and continued to stare, so I tried to conceal my embarrassment with a commonplace remark.

"It's quite close in here, don't you think?" I muttered.

But this pleasantry too went unheeded. Bending forward, he brought his face up close to mine and, rubbing his long bony fingers vigorously, spoke in a low whisper.

"They *were* alive, weren't they?"

Before I realized what I was doing, I found myself nodding in agreement. This admission seemed to please him greatly.

"Would you like to hear the story of their past?" he asked suddenly.

"Their—their past—did you say?" I blurted out, unable to interpret the meaning of his query.

"Yes, their past. That's what I said," he repeated in the same low tone "Especially that of the old man with the white hair."

"But—but I don't understand," I began, pinching myself to make sure that I was awake, and feeling the pain. "Do—do you mean—the story of his past—since his youth?"

"Exactly," he replied emphatically with an odd smile. "Since the day he was only twenty-five years old." And with these words I suddenly found myself yearning desperately to hear the whole tale.

"By all means tell me the story," I urged impatiently, sitting on the edge of my seat. 'Tell it to me in full detail."

Thereupon, the old man smiled again and launched into the following story:

"I remember it all very vividly," he began, "even to the precise day my elder brother turned into *that!*" He nodded toward the tablet. "It was on the evening of April 27, in 1895. . . . But let me start from the beginning.

"My brother and I were born the sons of a draper, living in the Nihonbashi district of downtown Tokyo. The time of which I speak was not long after they had built in Asakusa Park that twelve-story tower known as the Junikai which, until its destruction in the Great Earthquake, was a marvel of architecture for all provincial visitors to the capital. Almost every day my brother used to go and visit the tower, for he was of a very curious disposition and loved all things of foreign origin. These binoculars—yes, the ones you used—were but one example of this peculiar craze of his. He bought the binoculars at a small curio shop located in Yokohama's Chinatown. I remember my brother telling me that they had once belonged to the master of some foreign ship, and that he had paid a tidy sum for them."

Every time he said "my brother," the old man either looked or pointed at the other old man in the pasted rag picture, as if to emphasize his presence there. I soon realized that he identified the memories of his real brother with the white-haired old man in the picture, and hence talked as if the picture also were alive and listening to his story. Strangely enough, the fact did not strike me as being at all unusual. During those moments both of us must have been living in some strange domain far beyond the operations of the laws of nature.

"Did you ever go up the Junikai?" the old man's voice droned on. "No? What a pity. It was quite a strange building, I must say. I often used to wonder what sort of a wizard had built it. It was said to have been designed by an Italian architect.

"I must explain that in those days Asakusa Park was even more of a show place than it is now. At nearly every turn there was one attraction after another. To cite but a few, there was the Spider Man, a sword-dance show by a group of young girls, a noted circus entertainer with his favorite feat of dancing atop a ball, and peep shows galore. Then there was also the Puzzle Labyrinth, where you could easily get lost in a maze of paths partitioned by knitted bamboo screens.

"And finally, of course, there was the Tower, built of brick, rising abruptly from the center of the district. It was a dizzy two hundred and sixteen feet high—almost half a city block—and its octagonal top was shaped like a Chinese cap. Wherever you happened to be in Tokyo you could almost always see the Junikai.

"In the spring of 1895, not long after my brother had bought the binoculars, a strange thing happened to him. My father even thought that my brother was going mad, and worried about him constantly. As for myself, because I loved my brother deeply, I too could not help being sorely puzzled over his strange behavior. For days on end my brother took little food, hardly spoke a word to his family, and shut himself up in his room most of the time when he was at home.

"Before long he became thinner and thinner, while his face turned deadly pale, with only the eyes glaring brightly. Nevertheless, he was out from noon till evening each day, as regularly as if he was employed in some office. And whenever he was asked where he went, he would close his lips tightly and refuse to reply.

"My mother too worried over his strange habits and tried in every possible way to make him tell her the reason for his low spirits, but all to no avail. This state of affairs lasted for about a month.

"At last, I became so anxious to know where he went that one day I followed him secretly. On this particular day, too, it was cloudy and muggy, just like today. As had become his custom, it was a little past noon when my brother went out, clad in his smart black velvet suit, with his prized binoculars dangling from his shoulder.

"Following him at a safe distance, I saw him hurrying down the road leading to the horse-tramway stop at Nihonbashi. A moment later he got on an Asakusa-bound horsecar. As the cars ran rather infrequently, it was impossible for me to follow him in the next car. So I quickly hailed a rickshaw.

"'Quick! Follow that horsecar!' I ordered.

"The rickshawman proved fleet of foot and was able to keep the horsecar within sight with ease. Arriving at Asakusa Park, I saw my brother get off. I dismissed the rickshaw and continued to follow him on foot. And where do you think he finally arrived? At the Kwannon Temple in Asakusa Park.

"Unaware that he was being followed, my brother threaded his way through the crowds along the red-fronted shopping street, passed the main building of the temple, and then proceeded, through an even thicker throng converged around the show-booths at the rear, to the Junikai.

"He walked purposefully up to the stone gate, paid his admission fee, and disappeared into the tower. I, of course, was completely astonished, for I had never dreamed that my brother had been coming to this familiar landmark day after day. Young as I was—I was still in my teens then—I even thought that my brother might have been possessed by some evil spirit inhabiting the tower.

"For myself, I had climbed it only once, with my father, and never after that, so I felt rather uneasy about going in again. But, since my brother had gone in, I had no choice but to enter and go up the dark, stone stairs after him, keeping a safe distance behind. The windows were small and the brick wall was thick, so it was cool inside, just like a cave. On one wall hung several macabre war paintings done in oils—it was the time of the Sino-Japanese War.

"Higher and higher rose the gloomy stairway, just like the spiraling grooves in the shell of a snail. At the top of the tower there was a balcony, with a railing running around the edge. When I finally reached the balcony my eyes were dazzled by the sudden brightness, because the narrow, winding passage from the ground had been long and dark. Above me, the clouds were hanging low—so low, in fact, that I felt I could almost reach up with my hands and touch them.

"When I looked around, I saw all the roofs of Tokyo in a weird jumble, while on the distant horizon I could clearly make out the Bay of Tokyo. Directly below me I saw the Kwannon Temple, looking like a doll's house, and the many show-booths. As for the people, they all looked as if they had only heads and feet.

"Close beside me, I saw about ten other spectators huddled close together admiring the view. My brother stood apart from them, gazing eagerly at the compound of Asakusa Park through his binoculars. As I watched him from behind, I noted that his black velvet clothes stood out in sharp relief against the gray clouds. He looked so much like a figure in a Western oil-painting—austere and saintly—that for a moment I even hesitated to call out to him, although I well knew that he was really my brother.

"Remembering my mission, however, I couldn't remain silent. Going up to him, I asked abruptly: 'What are you looking at, brother?'

"He started, then wheeled around with a look of extreme annoyance.

"'Your recent strange behavior is causing Father and Mother untold anxiety,' I continued. 'We've all been wondering where you go every day. But now I know. You come here. But why, Brother, why? For God's sake, you've got to tell me. You can trust me, can't you?' On and on I pleaded with him.

"At first he refused to discuss the matter, but I kept pestering him for an explanation so insistently that he finally gave in. But even after he explained I found myself more mystified than ever, for what he said was altogether incomprehensible.

"According to him, one day about a month before, he happened to be gazing down through his binoculars from the top of the Junikai into the compound of the Kwannon Temple, when he had suddenly caught a glimpse of a girl's face amidst the crowds of people. She had been so beautiful, he explained—so uncannily beautiful—that he had been swept completely off his feet. For him, this sudden infatuation was a new sensation, for normally he was quite indifferent to feminine charms.

"But in his surprise and excitement, he had moved the binoculars too sharply. Frantically, he had brought the lenses back into focus, but by this time the face had vanished, and look as he might, he could not find it again.

"Ever since that moment my brother had not known a moment's peace—for the beautiful face of the girl kept haunting him, even in his dreams. And of course, it was the sad, forlorn hope of trying to find the girl in the temple compound that had caused my brother to waste away with complete disregard for any thought of food—and to keep climbing the Junikai day after day with his binoculars to scan the sea of faces below him.

"After finishing his confession, my brother went back to his binoculars in a frenzy of undying hope. Watching him, my heart bled with sympathy. He was indeed like the man looking for a needle in a haystack.

"To my way of thinking, his search was utterly futile, but I did not have the heart to disillusion him. Tears welling in my eyes, I continued to gaze at his pathetic figure.

"A few moments drifted by, and then gradually I became keenly aware of the beauty of the scene spread before my eyes. With my brother's slim figure outlined sharply against the sailing clouds, it appeared as if his body were floating in the air.

"Suddenly, a large number of colored balls, some dyed a deep blue, others in green, red, purple, and other lively hues, floated up into the sky, fashioning a fantastic design. I quickly leaned over the railings, and looking down saw that the strange phenomenon had not been the product of my imagination. It had so happened that a vendor of colored toy balloons had accidentally tipped over his stand, releasing all his stock in trade.

"Just at this moment, my brother broke into my reverie with a voice trembling with excitement.

"'Come—we've got to hurry, or we'll be too late!' he fairly screamed, pulling me roughly by the hand.

"As I ran after him down the stone stairway of the tower, I called out to him, asking what had happened.

"'The girl! The girl!' he cried. 'I've found her!'

"After reaching the ground, he seized my hand again and began to drag me with him as he made for the compound of the temple.

"'My search is over,' he gasped as he ran. I just saw her . . . sitting in a large room floored with straw mats. I know I can locate her now. I must! I must!'

"Going into greater detail as we hurried along, my brother explained that he was now seeking a landmark in the form of a tall pine tree, which he had seen through the binoculars, located somewhere at the rear of the Kwannon Temple. 'And near it,' he stammered excitedly, 'there is a house. She's there . . . there . . . !'

"We soon located the pine tree in question, but great was my brother's disappointment at finding not even the remotest trace of a house in the vicinity. Although I was persuaded that my brother was suffering from some optical illusion, I nevertheless began to search for signs of the girl in the neighboring teahouses, for I truly and sincerely felt sorry for my lovesick brother.

"While carrying out my search, I must have drifted away from my brother, for when I turned a moment later he was nowhere in sight. Hurrying back toward the pine tree, I chanced to pass a row of stalls, among which was a roofless peep-show booth. And then, suddenly, I stopped running, for I found my brother peering intently into one of the peepholes.

"'What are you looking at?' I asked abruptly, tapping him on the shoulder.

"I will never forget the strange expression he wore when he turned around. His eyes were glassy and appeared to be gazing at some far-off scene. His voice sounded decidedly unreal.

"'Brother,' he sighed, 'the girl . . . is inside.'

"Immediately grasping the significance of his statement, I peered into the peephole he had indicated.

"As soon as I pressed my eyes against the hole, an attractive face fairly leaped into view. Instantly I recognized the features as belonging to Yaoya-Oshichi, a well-known heroine immortalized on the classical Kabuki stage in a tragic love drama.

"Gradually, as my eyes came into focus, I was able to observe the whole setting of the peep show. The picture, for such it was, depicted the attractive girl Oshichi leaning amorously against the lap of her lover Kichiza in a guest room of the Kichijo Temple. Studying the pair more closely, I discovered that they were nothing more than the two main characters of a pasted rag picture. But the sheer artistry of the workmanship amazed me.

"Oshichi especially was a masterpiece, so true to life in every minute detail. I wasn't surprised, therefore, to hear my brother remark behind me: 'I know the girl is only a rag-picture doll, pasted on one of many tablets, but I simply cannot afford to give her up! Oh, if only I could be like her lover Kichiza in the picture, and talk to her!'

"As though petrified, my brother stood there, lost to the world. I soon realized that he must have seen the picture in the peep show from the top of the Junikai, through the open top of the booth.

"It was getting quite dark by this time, and already the crowds were thinning out. In front of the peep show there were now only a couple of children, who seemed reluctant to leave. But, eventually, they too left the place.

"It had been cloudy ever since noon that day, and now the skies were threatening rain. Somewhere in the distance I heard the faint rumbling sound of thunder, and streaks of lightning flashed across the leaden skies. But my brother continued to stand immobile, staring—staring far, far away.

216

"Soon the darkness descended like a black veil. Close by, I caught the bright gas-lit illumination of a signboard advertising the dancing-on-a-ball show.

"Suddenly, my brother came to himself and clutched my arm.

"'I've an idea,' he exclaimed. 'Here, hold these binoculars the wrong way and keep gazing at me with the larger lenses pressed close to your eyes!'

"This was an odd request, to say the least.

"'But why?' I remonstrated.

"'Never mind why! Just do as I ask!' he shot back.

"Reluctantly I picked up the binoculars, for it was a distasteful task to me. Ever since I could remember, I had felt a revulsion for all optical instruments. Somehow they seemed wicked to me—binoculars which could make objects seem either small and distant or else uncannily close, or a microscope which could magnify a small worm into the dimensions of a monster. But, having no other choice, I carried out my brother's wish, though with serious misgivings.

"As soon as I looked at my brother through the wrong end of the binoculars, I found him reduced in size to a mere two feet, and seemingly standing about six meters away. And then, gradually, as I continued to gaze, I saw him become smaller and smaller. Soon he was only about a foot in height. But I was undisturbed, for I thought that he was merely moving further away from me—walking backwards.

"Suddenly, however, I started violently, for his small figure began to float up in the air. And then—presto!—he vanished into the darkness.

"You can well imagine how scared I was. Lowering the binoculars, I began to run around in circles, screaming: 'Brother! Brother! Where are you? Where are you?' But all my efforts to find him proved fruitless.

"And this is the way, my friend, that my brother made his completely unexpected and weird exit from this earth.

"Ever since that time I have regarded binoculars as instruments of terror. I am especially afraid of this particular pair. Although it may sound superstitious, I have always had the feeling that swift misfortune will overtake any man who looks through these lenses from the wrong end. Maybe you can now understand why I stopped you so violently when you held them the wrong way a few moments ago.

"To return to my story—I soon tired of my search and returned to the peep show. Suddenly, like a bolt from the blue, I was struck by an odd thought.

"'Could it be possible,' I asked myself with a shudder, 'that my brother purposely reduced himself in size by dint of the black magic of the wicked binoculars and went to join the girl of his undying affection in the pasted rag picture?'

"Jolted by this thought, I quickly aroused the owner of the booth and asked him to let me have another look at the picture slide of the Kichijo Temple. Sure enough, as soon as I saw the pasted rag picture by the light of an oil lamp, I found that the worst had come to pass. For there, in that fantastic setting, sat my brother instead of the character Kichiza, passionately hugging the gorgeous Oshichi.

"Strange to say, I did not feel any sadness or remorse. On the contrary, I was extremely happy to know that my brother had finally attained his long-cherished desire.

"After succeeding in negotiating with the peep-show owner for the sale of the picture to me—for some strange reason, he never noticed that my brother, clad in his Western suit, had usurped the role of Kichiza—I hurried home and told the whole story to my family. But of course no one believed me— not even my mother. They all thought that I had gone stark raving mad."

Concluding his story, the old man began to chuckle to himself. And for some unexplainable reason, I too found myself smiling.

"I could never convince them," he suddenly continued, "of the possibility of a man's turning into a rag-picture doll. But the very fact that my brother had completely vanished from the face of the earth proves that such is possible.

"My father, for example, still believes that my brother ran away from home. As for my mother, I finally succeeded in borrowing enough money from her to buy the tablet bearing the precious rag picture. Shortly after I journeyed to Hakone and Kamakura, carrying the picture with me, for I would not deny my beloved brother a honeymoon.

"Now you can well understand why I always prop the picture up against the window whenever I ride on a train, for it is always my desire to let him and his lover enjoy the passing scenery.

"Before long, my father liquidated his business in Tokyo and moved to his native city of Toyama. I too have lived there for the past thirty years. And then, a few days ago, I decided to let my brother enjoy the sights of the new Tokyo, and that is the reason why I am making this trip.

"Sad to say, however, there is just one setback to my brother's happiness, for while the girl always remains young and fresh—for she is actually nothing but a doll despite her lifelike features—my brother grows older and haggard with the passing of each year, for he is human, of flesh and blood, just as you and I. Where once he was a handsome and dashing young man of twenty-five, he has now been reduced to a whitehaired old man, feeble of limb and ugly with wrinkles.

"Ah! What a sad situation! And what irony!"

Sighing deeply, the old man straightened, as if he had suddenly awakened from a trance.

"Well, I've told a long story," he remarked. "And I assure you that every word I've spoken is true. You do believe me, don't you?"

"Of course, of course!" I reassured him.

"I am truly happy to know," he replied, "that my narrative has not been wasted."

He then turned to the rag picture, and began to speak in a soft voice, like the cooing of a dove:

"You must both be tired, my dear brother and sister-in-law. And you must also be feeling embarrassed, for I told the story in your presence. But cheer up, I'll put you to bed now."

With these words, he again wrapped the picture painstakingly in the cloth wrapper.

As he did this, I caught a fleeting glimpse of the faces of the two figures, and I could have sworn that they had thrown me a smile of friendly greeting. As for the old man, he had lapsed into silence.

On and on sped the train. About ten minutes later the tempo of the rumbling wheels grew slower, while a few scattered lights could now be seen glimmering outside the windows.

Shortly after, the train came to a halt at a small and obscure station high in the mountains. Looking out, I saw only one station clerk standing on the platform.

The old man got to his feet.

"I must now bid you farewell," he muttered. "This is where I must get off, for I am staying with relatives in this village tonight."

With these words, the old man hobbled down the aisle and stepped off the carriage, the mysterious parcel clutched tightly under his arm.

Gazing out the window, I caught a final glimpse of him handing his ticket to the clerk at the wicket, and a moment later he was swallowed into the night.

Selected Bibliography

Prepared by Patricia Welch

Angles, Jeffrey. 2008. "Seeking the Strange: *Ryoki* and the Navigation of Normality in Interwar Japan." *Monumenta Nipponica*, Vol. 63, No. 1: 101–141.

Gardner, William O. 2006. *Advertising Tower: Japanese Modernism and Modernity in the 1920s*. Cambridge: Harvard University Asia Center.

Igarashi, Yoshikuni. 2005. "Edogawa Rampo and the Excess of Vision: An Ocular Critique of Modernity in 1920s Japan." *Positions: East Asia Cultures Critique*, Volume 13, Number 2: 299–327.

Jacobowitz, Seth, translator and editor. Introduction by Tatsumi Takayuki. 2008. *The Edogawa Rampo Reader*. Fukuoka: Kurodahan Press.

Kawana, Sari. 2008. *Murder Most Modern: Detective Fiction and Japanese Culture*. Minneapolis: University of Minnesota Press.

King, Stephen. 1987. *Danse Macabre*. New York: Berkley Books.

Marling, William. 2003. "Vision and Putrescence: Edogawa Rampo Rereading Edgar Allen Poe." *Poe Studies/Dark Romanticism*.

Posadas, Baryon Tensor. 2010. *Double Fictions and Double Visions of Japanese Modernity*. Unpublished Dissertation. University of Toronto.

Reichert, Jim. 2001. "Deviance and Social Darwinism in Edogawa Ranpo's Erotic-Grotesque Thriller *Kotō no oni*." *Journal of Japanese Studies*, 27:1: 113~141.

Silver, Mark. 2008. *Purloined Letters: Cultural Borrowing and Japanese Crime Literature*, 1868–1937. Honolulu: University of Hawaii Press.

Tyler, William. 2008. *Modanizumu: Modernist Fiction from Japan, 1913–1938*. Honolulu: University of Hawaii Press.

TUTTLE CLASSICS

LITERATURE   (* = for sale in Japan only)

ABE, Kobo   安部公房
The Woman in the Dunes   砂の女   ISBN 978-4-8053-0900-1*

AKUTAGAWA, Ryunosuke   芥川龍之介
Kappa   河童   ISBN 978-4-8053-0901-8*
Rashomon and Other Stories   羅生門   ISBN 978-4-8053-0882-0

DAZAI, Osamu   太宰治
No Longer Human   人間失格   ISBN 978-4-8053-1017-5*

ENDO, Shusaku   遠藤周作
The Final Martyrs   最後の殉教者   ISBN 978-4-8053-0625-3*
The Golden Country 黄金の国   ISBN 978-0-8048-3337-0*

HEARN, Lafcadio   ラフカディオ・ハーン
Glimpses of Unfamiliar Japan   知られざる日本の面影
  ISBN 978-4-8053-1025-0
In Ghostly Japan   霊の日本   ISBN 978-0-8048-3661-6;
  978-4-8053-0749-6*
Kokoro 心   ISBN 978-0-8048-3660-9; 978-4-8053-0748-9*
Kwaidan 怪談   ISBN 978-0-8048-3662-3; 978-4-8053-0750-2*
Lafcadio Hearn's Japan   ラフカディオ・ハーンの日本
  ISBN 978-4-8053-0873-8

INOUE, Yasushi   井上靖
The Samurai Banner of Furin Kazan   風林火山
  ISBN 978-0-8048-3701-9; 978-4-8053-0910-0*

KAWABATA, Yasunari   川端康成
The Izu Dancer and Other Stories   伊豆の踊り子
  ISBN 978-4-8053-0744-1*
The Master of Go   名人   ISBN 978-4-8053-0673-4*
The Old Capital   古都   ISBN 978-4-8053-0972-8*
Snow Country 雪国   ISBN 978-4-8053-0635-2*

MISHIMA, Yukio 三島由紀夫

Five Modern Noh Plays 近代能楽集 ISBN 978-4-8053-1032-8*

The Temple of the Golden Pavilion 金閣寺
ISBN 978-4-8053-0637-6*

NATSUME, Soseki 夏目漱石

And Then それから ISBN 978-0-8048-1537-6; 978-4-8053-1141-7*

Botchan 坊ちゃん ISBN 978-0-8048-3703-3; 978-4-8053-1263-6*

Grass on the Wayside 道草 ISBN 978-4-8053-0258-3*

I am a Cat 吾輩は猫である ISBN 978-0-8048-3265-6;
978-4-8053-1097-7*

Kokoro こころ ISBN 978-4-8053-0746-5*

TANIZAKI, Junichiro 谷崎潤一郎

In Praise of Shadows 陰翳礼賛 ISBN 978-4-8053-0665-9*

The Key 鍵 ISBN 978-4-8053-0632-1*

The Makioka Sisters 細雪 ISBN 978-4-8053-0670-3*

Naomi 痴人の愛 ISBN 978-0-8048-1520-8; 978-4-8053-0622-2*

Some Prefer Nettles 蓼喰う虫 ISBN 978-4-8055-0633-8*

OTHERS

Donald Richie Memoirs of the Warrior Kumagai 熊谷直実
ISBN 978-4-8053-0847-9*

EDOGAWA, Rampo Japanese Tales of Mystery & Imagination
乱歩短編集 ISBN 978-0-8048-0319-9; 978-4-8053-1193-6

John Allyn The 47 Ronin Story 四十七士
ISBN 978-0-8048-3827-6: 978-4-8053-0871-4*

NOSAKA, Akiyuki The Pornographers エロ事師たち
ISBN 978-4-8053-0646-8*

OE, Kenzaburo A Personal Matter 個人的な体験
ISBN 978-4-8053-0641-3*

Richard Neery Japanese Mistress 二号さん
ISBN 978-4-8053-0654-7*